A twig cracked underfoot...

Matt curled his thumb around the hammer of his sidearm and drew it back, the *click-click* sounding loud in the night. Whoever they were, they were coming in.

They stood pressed against the trees. Glancing over his shoulder, Matt could see the glint of the moon on the rifle barrels of a half-dozen men lying prone in a shallow gulley.

His eyes swept the prairie, examining each shadow, each low, formless mass.

All was deathly still.

And suddenly they charged, as if rising out of the earth...

EASY COMPANY

EASY AND THE HEADLINE HUNTER COMPANY

JOHN WESLEY HOWARD

A JOVE BOOK

First Jove edition published November 1981

First printing

Printed in the United States of America

Jove books are published by Jove Publications, Inc., 200 Madison Avenue, New York, NY 10016

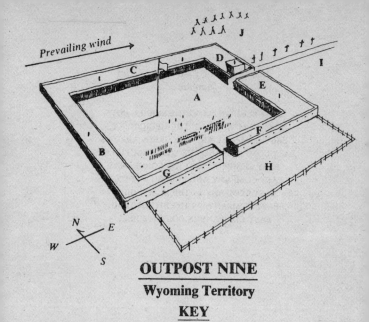

OUTPOST NINE
Wyoming Territory
KEY

A. Parade and flagstaff

B. Officers' quarters ("officers' country")

C. Enlisted men's quarters: barracks, day room, and mess

D. Kitchen, quartermaster supplies, ordnance shop, guardhouse

E. Suttler's store and other shops, tack room, and smithy

F. Stables

G. Quarters for dependents and guests; communal kitchen

H. Paddock

I. Road and telegraph line to regimental headquarters

J. Indian camp occupied by transient "friendlies"

INTERIOR   OUTSIDE

OUTPOST NUMBER NINE
(DETAIL)

Outpost Number Nine is a typical High Plains military outpost of the days following the Battle of the Little Big Horn, and is the home of Easy Company. It is not a "fort"; an official fort is the headquarters of a regiment. However, it resembles a fort in its construction.

The birdseye view shows the general layout and orientation of Outpost Number Nine; features are explained in the Key.

The detail shows a cross-section through the outpost's double walls, which ingeniously combine the functions of fortification and shelter.

The walls are constructed of sod, dug from the prairie on which Outpost Number Nine stands, and are sturdy enough to withstand an assault by anything less than artillery. The roof is of log beams covered by planking, tarpaper, and a top layer of sod. It also provides a parapet from which the outpost's defenders can fire down on an attacking force.

EASY
AND THE
HEADLINE
HUNTER

COMPANY

one

The gray rain slanted down in the predawn. Captain Warner Conway stood at the window, watching as a bridge of bone-white lightning exploded across the skies of Wyoming, briefly illuminating the severe, familiar lines of Outpost Number Nine.

It was exactly a half-hour before reveille. He knew that without glancing at the brass clock on the table beside the bed where Flora was stirring. Years of rising at the same hour had tuned Conway's body clock to a preciseness that a mere mechanical gadget could never achieve.

It was not going to be a good day. The rain wouldn't last long, but it would probably erase any tracks Elk Tooth and his band of hostiles might have left for Windy Mandalian and Lieutenant Taylor.

The cagy Cheyenne had been having himself a fine romp across the territory, lifting a scalp here and there, bringing in the usual storm of complaints and demands for action.

Elk Tooth was a renegade. When times had been tough, in the winter cold he had ridden into the Indian agency and, laying down his lance, vowed his loyalty to President Hayes.

After wintering up at agency expense, filling his belly by the fire, and getting himself and his men equipped with those damned Spencer repeaters, Elk Tooth had had a change of heart.

It was the new grass for his war ponies, which he saw growing across the spring prairie, the feel of a good rifle in his hand. He decided that Hayes was far away and hadn't done much for him lately. So Elk Tooth had ridden off, his war bonnet perched on his head, his dark little heart pounding with exultation.

1

Conway turned back toward the bed. Flora was sitting up, extending her arms overhead, her mouth stretched into a mighty yawn.

When she was finished with that ritual, she managed a smile and a perky "Good morning."

"It's raining," Conway said, crossing to the bed.

Flora frowned and glanced up at the roof, knowing it would leak. It always did. Sod laid over planking, with tarpaper sandwiched in between. There was always a deal of mud on the bed and the desk in the corner, and near the door.

"Will it last?" she asked.

"It looks like it's clearing already," Conway answered, sitting beside his wife. She stretched out a hand and touched his cheek, that tender, giving little smile on her lips.

"There were times when we were younger, Warner."

"I was just thinking about that. Days it would rain and we would spend the time in bed, watching the rain trickle down the windows. Long ago."

"Not so long, she objected.

No, but I wasn't CO in those days."

Flora Conway took a deep breath. "CO of a half-manned, godforsaken post," she said, imitating his deeper voice. Captain Conway laughted, kissed his wife, and stood.

"Unfortunately it's all true."

"I know it is, Captain," Flora nodded. She swung her legs from beneath the quilt and slapped her husband on the ass. "So get your butt in gear, Conway."

Conway frowned reflexively, then allowed himself a brief smile. He didn't particularly care for Flora's talking that way. But then, what the hell, it was hard to dislike anything that woman did, impossible to hold a grudge.

A large drop of reddish mud plopped square in the middle of the bed, staining the quilt as Flora watched. She clucked a little and shoved the bed to the middle of the room, away from the drip.

Captain Conway lathered up some soap in his shaving cup and brushed the lather onto his throat and tanned cheeks. He brushed the razor with practiced strokes along the strop that hung beside the mirror and carefully shaved his face to a shiny smoothness.

His thoughts were with Taylor and Windy Mandalian. They were rising to a bitter day out in the field, mud and slop and hostiles. Flora was whistling as she dressed, and that was a cheerful sound. Still, Conway couldn't shake the notion that it was going to be a bad day.

Reb McBride was sure of it. He stood under the eaves on the porch of the enlisted men's quarters, miserably eyeing the rain. He wore a slicker and carried his bugle beneath it, glancing at the silver pocket watch he had inherited from his grandfather.

There was no one on the parade but Reb; the flag wouldn't be run up unless this rain stopped. He watched the hand on that watch move up one mark, and then Reb clicked the cover shut.

Reveille sounded clear and diligent above the rain. Reb thrust the bugle back inside his rain slicker and took one more miserable glance at the rain, at the smoke that rose from the mess hall chimney, swirling around briefly before being smothered by the storm.

Reb scraped his boots and scuffled into the barracks. Stretch was sitting on the end of his bunk like an unopened jackknife, and he glanced up, blinking sleepily.

Holzer was already dressed, his hair slicked back, a smile on his face. He clicked his heels at Reb. Reb threw his hat down in disgust and then peeled his slicker. He stood for a long minute, staring at the stove.

"What the hell's the matter with him?" Malone asked.

"It's Rothausen." Stretch Dobbs yawned. He stood and stretched those long arms, arms that seemed to spread across the width of the room. Dobbs was all of six and a half feet tall, narrowly built, most often wearing an expression of faint puzzlement.

"What about Rothausen?" Corporal Wojensky asked. He slid his galluses up over his shoulders and looked from Reb to Stretch and back.

"Hell," Reb drawled, "if you don't know...."

"He's got an iron gut. Iron-gut Wojensky," Malone spat.

"Somebody tell me what the hell you're talking about?" Wojensky pleaded.

"Jesus, Wojensky," Reb said, waving his hands in the air. "Don't you know? Really? It's Rothausen's food. It's crap lately. Crap!"

"I thought it was all right," Wojensky said hesitantly. Reb groaned and Malone chimed in.

"They're right, you know," Stretch agreed. "Somebody ought to say something to him."

"Are you crazy? He'd bend your skull with a rolling pin."

"Well then, the first shirt should be told. Somebody ought to have a talk with Ben Cohen."

"Cohen knows," Reb said in sheer exasperation. "He has to. The trouble is, it's not something Rothausen's doing on purpose. I mean he just don't have his head on straight."

"He needs a piece of ass," Malone decided finally.

"Who don't?" Stretch replied.

"Don't even mention it. I don't want to think about it."

"Yeah, but Rothausen—I mean he *really* needs it," Malone insisted. "And it's not that easy to find him a woman."

"It ain't that easy for *anybody* to find a woman," Reb said. "It ain't that easy to find *anything*. But Christ, at least we used to eat good."

"You're right, dead right," Malone said.

"It just ain't right for one man to have so much power," Reb considered. He glanced again at his watch, and picking up his hat, he smoothed it and went back out into the drizzle to blow grub call.

"You coming, Holzer?" Wojensky asked, slinging his gunbelt around his hips.

"Yes!" Holzer said brightly. He was standing at perfect attention. Wojensky looked at him for a minute, trying to decide if Holzer understood the question. He was an amazing one, Wolfie. Signed up on the docks as he stepped from a ship, Wolfgang Holzer never had really understood just how he got into the army—maybe he thought every American had to serve his military time when requested.

Odd thing about Wolfie was that he went at it all with

4

eagerness and dynamic motion. If only he knew what folks were talking about.

Wojensky put his hat on, peered into the mirror, folded up his hat brim, and nodded to Holzer. "Let's go, Wolfie. How about you, Cutter?"

Cutter Grimes glanced up from his bunk. His open blue eyes focused on Wojensky finally, and he shook his head.

"What's the matter, you sick?" the corporal asked. Grimes just shook his head. He sat there polishing his brass belt buckle, and his eyes hardly lifted.

Wojensky sighed and slapped his thighs. "Everybody's getting sulky."

"Leave him be, Wojensky," Stretch said. He nodded his head furtively, and Wojensky, seeing that something was up, angled his hat and followed Wolfie and Stretch out. He nearly bumped into Reb, who was returning to the barracks.

"You were serious? You're not going to eat?"

"I'm serious. When he serves shit-on-a-shingle these days, that's exactly what it is."

Wojensky shook his head, glanced up at the clearing skies, and went on toward the mess hall. Reb went into the barracks, shaking out his slicker, which he hung on the peg beside his bunk. Grimes was the only other man there.

"What's up, Cutter?"

"Same thing, Reb."

"Yeah?" Reb McBride took off his hat and sailed it to his bunk. Then he sat opposite Cutter, watching as the blue-eyed kid lethargically polished his buckle. "No way out?" Reb asked.

"No. I ain't gonna make it," Cutter said, lifting those eyes, which, except for their color, might have belonged to a hound dog.

Cutter Grimes had a big problem and he had the dismals. He was due to be discharged in two weeks, but he wasn't going to be. He had debts with Pop Evans, the sutler, and by regulation they had to be cleared before a man could be given his discharge papers.

"Didn't you know, Cutter? Damn, Pop has that copy of the ARs hanging right behind his counter."

"I know he does," Cutter said mournfully. "It's my own

5

fault. Guess I'll be hanging around Outpost Nine for a while, Reb."

"What about that girl of yours?" Reb asked. Cutter didn't answer. Trouble with Cutter was the West Virginian had too soft a heart. He had sent his pay home to his folks, and a chunk of it to his girl. Then he had gotten his credit stretched pretty damned thin at the sutler's. Word was that Cutter had tried to make it all up at once, plopping down all he had in town on a single spin of the Wheel of Fortune. Now he had nothing.

"Maybe I'll make corporal next hitch."

"Hell, brighten up, Cutter." Reb grinned broadly. "This ain't the first time this has happened. The boys'll help you."

"They cain't," Cutter said. Finally he had that belt buckle polished to his satisfaction. He stood and slipped it on.

"Sure we can. Look, how much do you owe Pop Evans, anyway?"

"Three hundred dollars."

He said it softly, and at first Reb thought he hadn't heard him right. He cocked his head, as if that would clear his ears. He stared at Cutter, his jaw sagging slightly.

"Did I hear that right?"

"Three hundred dollars," Cutter repeated in the same hound-dog tone.

"It's impossible"

"Sure is," Cutter said. He picked up his rifle and nodded. "B'lieve I'll check the duty roster."

"Wait!" Reb grabbed his arm, positioning himself in front of Cutter. "Are you sure Pop said three hundred?"

"That's it, Reb. I guess it adds up. What with interest compounded and all. Pop explained all that compounding interest and such to me." Cutter rubbed his shoulder and shrugged. "It was all new to me. Interesting," he admitted, "but all a new twist on it to me."

"Listen, Cutter. Don't you give up now, hear?" Reb was sincere. Cutter only halfheartedly listened. "Like I say, this has happened before. You got a little girl waitin' to marry you. You'd rather be there than hanging around Outpost Nine playing games with Lo. Me and the boys," Reb promised him, "we'll help you. You just hang on."

"Sure. Thanks, Reb," Cutter said with a brief smile. Then he went on out into the chill morning. Reb watched him from the doorway for a minute, seeing clear, brilliant sunlight break through the leaden clouds. He caught a scent of breakfast on the wind and he grimaced.

"Jesus. Suffering Jesus," Reb said, shaking his head. What was that supposed to be? Dutch Rothausen was going mad in that kitchen, inventing new poisons as he went.

Glancing up, Reb saw Ben Cohen unlocking the orderly room and he headed that way, cutting across the muddy parade.

The orderly room was still chilly when Reb stepped in. Acting Master Sergeant Ben Cohen sat at his desk, his eyes slightly glazed, his massive jaw clenched. He looked exactly like an angry, clean-shaven grizzly, and Reb hesitated a moment.

"What the hell do you want?" Cohen asked. He had a hand on his belly and he snapped his words off.

"Rothausen?" Reb asked.

"What's with him? Is he crazy?" Cohen stood and stalked across the floor, taking the blue enamel coffeepot from the iron stove. He poured a cup and offered one to Reb.

"Have you talked to him about it, Sarge?"

"Talked to him?" Cohen's voice was oddly soft for a moment. "I told him I'd punch his face through the back of his head if he didn't straighten it out. This army's not traveling very far on its belly with Rothausen in charge of cooking. Damn—and he used to be a fair hand." Cohen sagged into his chair, hunkering over his coffee.

He lifted his eyes to the bugler. "I chewed his ass up one side and down the other, Reb. What does he do? He smiles and nods. 'Thanks, Ben,' he says."

"It's the lack of pussy," Reb said.

"What?"

"It's Malone's theory. Something about the congestion of the gonads."

"Malone has congestion of the brain. Hell, anybody who treats his stomach the way Malone does, what's he know?"

7

"I don't know. Something's got to be done before Roth-ausen gets busted or somebody goes down with ptomaine."

"Yeah." They sat there in silence for a time. Cohen had his beefy hands wrapped around his coffee cup. Reb was trying to decide how to word what he had to say. Finally he simply asked.

"How much is in the slush fund, Sarge?"

"What do you want to do, bribe Rothausen to cook a decent meal?"

"No. It's something else. Cutter Grimes. He doesn't want to re-up, but it looks like he might have to."

Cohen's eyebrows lifted slightly. "Go on."

"Pop Evans's got a hold on him, Sarge. A good strong hold. That's why I'm askin'."

"Well, there should be something. How much does he need?"

Reb told him, and he used the same mumbling tone that Cutter had when mentioning the figure. "Three hundred dollars."

"Three hundred!"

Cohen had been looking into the tin box where he kept the slush fund, and now he slammed the lid shut and came to his feet, hovering over Reb. "Did you say three hundred dollars or not, Reb?"

"Three hundred."

"That's . . . what is that, sixteen month's pay? How?"

"Something to do with compound interest," Reb shrugged.

"You want to do that boy a favor?" Cohen said, pointing a stubby finger in Reb's direction. "Talk him into loving the army, the mounted infantry, and Outpost Nine. Because he's going to be with us a long time, Reb. A long damn time."

Cohen shook his head. He waved his hand, indicating that as far as he was concerned there was no use discussing it any further. Reb finished his coffee, replaced the cup, and went on out, just catching the front end of a long and profuse curse from behind him in Cohen's office.

Cohen muttered it heavily. "I'll be a son of a . . ."

Reb came out as Captain Conway was striding toward the orderly room, and McBride snapped a salute. Conway responded, "Good morning, bugler," and passed by. He opened the door and caught the tail end of Cohen's elaborate oath.

". . . tick-thick, slavering bitch." Cohen felt the cool draft and his eyes flickered to the door. He came to his feet, his face flushing sheepishly. "Good morning, sir."

"Good morning. What's the stimulation, Sergeant Cohen?"

"I think maybe you'd like a cup of coffee first," Cohen said. He held a dispatch in his hand and the captain nodded.

"All right. Bring them together," Conway agreed. "Any word from Taylor?"

"None, sir."

Conway nodded. That was to be expected. He doubted seriously that even Windy Mandalian would find a trace of Elk Tooth after that rain. He walked into his office, hanging his hat as he passed the hat tree. A portrait of President Hayes hung behind his desk now, and on that desk was a trophy Matt Kincaid had brought in: a red stone pipe wrapped in rawhide, decorated with feathers. A Cheyenne had told Matt that it was the one he had shared with Sitting Bull at Greasy Grass. The Litte Big Horn.

The door opened and Cohen entered with a cup of black, bitter coffee and the morning's mail. He handed the papers to the captain without comment, but Cohen's face indicated that there was something in the dispatches that Captain Conway would find distasteful.

And there was. It was right on top, evidently the motivator of Cohen's fluent curse. Conway had much the same reaction to it.

He read the dispatch once, then again. Then, rising, he went to his office door and called to Cohen, "Have Lieutenant Kincaid report to me, Sergeant."

Kincaid must have already been on his way, for it wasn't three minutes before the lieutenant came in. Conway waved his adjutant toward a chair.

"You look a little bemused, Warner. Elk Tooth again?"

"Nothing so soft, Matt." He pushed the dispatch to Kincaid's side of the desk, and the lieutenant read it, frowning deeply.

"That's about all we need right now," Kincaid said, "A

9

damned newspaper reporter. And what do you think he'll be looking for?"

"Anything sensational," Captain Conway guessed. "Oh, I shouldn't start hanging flags on the man before I've met him. But I've dealt with newspapermen before, Matt. Or tried to. Enough to discover that public relations is not my forte."

"Bates DeQueen," Matt said, reading the name from the dispatch. "You ever heard of him?"

"No." Conway shook his head. "But I've heard plenty of that *New York Herald* and that James Gordon Bennett who runs it. If we trip up, talking to this DeQueen, half the country's going to hear us when we fall."

"What's the advice from HQ?" Kincaid wanted to know.

"The advice is—and this comes all the way down from the top echelon of War, Matt—'present a positive image.'" He read, "It is imperative that Bates DeQueen, and through him the vast readership of the *New York Herald*, receives a positive image of the War Department's efforts on the Western Plains. However, a considerable amount of caution will have to be exercised." Conway looked up. "You've read it. What do you think they want, exactly?"

"I think," Matt grinned, "they want to lay it on our shoulders, sir. Give this newspaperman full, guarded cooperation. Give him a good impression of a bad situation." Matt was no longer grinning. "I think I can feel an ax hanging over us somewhere up there."

"Well, we'll charge on, Matt. We'll put up with this man, react civilly to his questions. In a month or two we'll have forgotten he was ever here."

"And we can hope that too," Matt said.

"Yes." Conway was thoughtfully silent for a minute. Then he rose. "That's about it. The man is arriving this afternoon. I can't imagine where this got held up. Or maybe they simply didn't want us to have much advance warning."

He had walked Matt Kincaid to the door, and now Captain Conway told Ben Cohen, "Sergeant, let's get those barracks scrubbed up. Only necessary details in the field."

"Yessir."

Cohen snatched up his hat and was gone. Matt shook his

10

head once and was gone as well. Captain Conway stood in the doorway for a minute, looking to the skies, where the clearing clouds drifted eastward.

"A newspaperman." He wagged his head and returned to his office.

Cohen found Corporal Miller at the smith's shed and had him pass the word to the other squad leaders. Those barracks *will* be clean.

There were a few other items. The visiting officers' quarters would have to be cleaned up a bit, fresh linen on the bed. Maggie could take care of that. This DeQueen would likely be dining with the captain and Mrs. Conway . . . wouldn't he?

Cohen stopped in his tracks for a minute. Then, walking faster, he veered sharply toward the mess hall. If this DeQueen had the influence the captain thought he had, they were in trouble, and it went right up the line before inertia stopped it and it began to come back down. Shit does roll downhill. If Mr. DeQueen didn't have a decent meal, why was that, Captain?

Inevitably it became, "Why didn't DeQueen have a decent meal, Sergeant Cohen, if you knew something was wrong with Rothausen?"

Ben Cohen should have said something to the captain, but he hadn't. He figured Rothausen would snap out of it sooner or later, preferably before the captain made one of his usual visits to the mess, eating with the men, which he hadn't done for some time.

The thing was, Dutch was a good cook. He truly was. A fat, storming pain in the ass, maybe, at times, but he had more ways to cook buffalo and 'desecrated potatoes' and make it taste good than a man would believe. And he had been a good hand with cakes and dried-apple pies. You could always count on finding fresh coffee ready at Rothausen's mess hall.

Previously.

Ben stepped into the mess hall, empty now but for Blackwell, who was doing KP, and would be for a time longer, as punishment for that pig race in town.

11

Cohen reached for the kitchen door and then leaped back, just in time to miss the flying, wide-eyed figure of Private James J. Dooley, followed by the voice of Rothausen, which sounded like the roar of a gored grizzly.

Cohen stepped around a dazed Dooley, and with his own blood starting to rise, he went into the kitchen where Dutch was storming from pot rack to pot rack, tearing the copper pots from their hooks.

"If the son of a bitch would clean them..." Dutch panted. Then his eyes settled on Cohen, who stood there, hands on hips, eyeing Rothausen steadily, impatiently.

"Dutch." Ben Cohen went to the cook and took the pot the big man held in his hand, setting it aside. Dutch smelled nervous. His eyes were nervous eyes. His hands shook.

"You're a mess, Dutch."

Rothausen waved a long wooden spoon at the first sergeant. "I don't need you butting in, Ben."

"I butt in where it's needed, Dutch, and you damned well know it."

"And my kitchen needs it?"

"That's right," Ben told him.

"It's the help I get, Ben," Dutch moaned. He leaned his bulk up against the wall. Something that did smell good was boiling away in a huge pot. "These temporary KP men. They don't give a damn. Look at this." He leaned over, picked up a copper kettle, and showed Cohen where the KPs had missed polishing a silver-dollar-sized piece of copper.

"I'm trying to get you a new assistant," Cohen said. He looked Dutch over once more, coming to the same conclusion. The big man was a mess. Fat and loose meat held together only by his big white apron. A bundle of spasmodic nerves.

"But it's not only that I came to talk about."

Dutch glanced around. "No?" He scooped two cups of salt into the pot. It was buffalo stew, and at least that seemed to be doing all right. "What is it, then?" Dutch demanded.

Now they were at the critical point. How did he tell him his food was no damned good? He didn't want to get into a fistfight with Dutch, and they didn't need him going off

12

on a sulk. Ben sucked it up and told him flat out.

"It's your meals lately, Dutch. They're bad. Damned bad."

"I haven't heard any complaints," Dutch said, "but yours."

"Who would complain to your face?" Ben asked, and Rothausen nodded, comprehending the logic of that. Dutch was fat, but he was strong and, aside from Ben Cohen, there probably wasn't a man on the post who could take him in a knuckle-and-fist contest.

"I got a fair idea of what I'm doing here," Dutch said with a tight little smile. "There's no problem. Maybe it's your taste buds." He took another scoop of salt from the bag and poured it into the stew pot.

"Are you supposed to do that twice?" Ben asked.

"Do what?"

"Salt it twice."

"Hell no, I wouldn't salt it twice," Dutch said, and he came erect, his jaw set. Cohen waved a hand, calming him down.

Ben sighed, looking at the stew, which was likely too salty to be eaten now. "Listen to me, Dutch. I'm trying to do you a favor. You got men complaining all over the post. We got a bugler who gags when he has to blow grub call. It can't be long before the captain gets wind of this. And then your ass is going to be on the carpet. I'd hate to see you get busted, Dutch, or lose this kitchen." Cohen glanced around as if he could already see the kitchen slipping away.

"We've got a VIP due in this afternoon. Whatever the hell's bothering you, Dutch, get it straightened out."

Rothausen was shaking with anger, his neck flushing red. He gripped that wooden spoon as though he wanted to strangle it to splinters. Then that mood slowly faded and he looked at Cohen with sincerity.

"I'll try, Ben. I don't know what the hell the problem is. I didn't know there was one. Thanks for telling me."

"No problem." Ben nodded. "That's my job."

Then he turned and walked out of the battle-littered kitchen. Glancing back over his shoulder, he saw a diligent Dutch Rothausen salting the stew again.

Gritting his teeth, Ben stalked out of the mess hall. There would be no stew worth eating tonight. Coming into the crystal daylight, he glanced up and across the parade, seeing the sutler, Pop Evans, roll out a barrel of crackers.

That reminded Cohen of Cutter Grimes and his problem. But that would have to wait awhile. Cohen had much to do before this DeQueen arrived. There was a new recruit due in as well, possibly on the same coach as DeQueen.

What was that soldier's name? Ben fumbled with his memory for a bit before he found it. Torkleson, private.

He wondered vaguely if Private Torkleson had ever had any cooking experience.

Just for a moment, Cohen stopped and looked toward the plains, where Taylor and his patrol were stalking Elk Tooth. Right now that seemed like a fine place to be. With nothing but Cheyenne and Sioux, hard weather and saddle sores to worry about.

two ────────────

It was Windy Mandalian who circled out wide, checking the sad heap of ashes, blackened timbers, and scorched iron that had been a prairie schooner. The patrol saw Windy step down and circle the wagon, his rifle across his arm.

Lieutenant Taylor sat his bay rigidly. The horse bowed its head to pull at the rain-freshened grama grass. It was a time before Windy came back in and reported. Taylor had read it on his face already, however, and the scout's words only reinforced what he already knew.

"Civilians," Windy said, his dark eyes fixed on Taylor's. "Man, woman, and boy child. Man had his fingers trimmed, scalp lifted. The old lady had her skirt up over her face. The kid had his skull bashed in. They went through their trunk, clothes and linen's scattered around."

"Elk Tooth?"

Windy shrugged. "I can't read him by that, but he's the only Cheyenne I know of that's kicking up his heels right now."

"Where's he heading, Windy?" Taylor's eyes swept the far horizons. He watched the grass quiver in the wind that blew in gusts, following the storm. It gave the illusion of a sea, of a trembling earth.

"Maybe to the mountains. Camas Meadows?" Windy shrugged. "I can't figure him, Taylor. He's runnin' crazy, seems like. But whatever path he chooses"—Windy nodded toward the burned-out wagon—"it'll be a bloody trail."

"I'll need a burial detail," Taylor said to Corporal Wilson, who sat his horse beside him.

"Yessir."

15

Taylor watched as they rode toward the wagon, the wind in his face, the horse shuddering beneath him. Then he lifted his eyes again to the far horizon.

"I hope to Christ there's nobody else in Elk Tooth's path," Taylor said. Windy looked up, his dark face nodding agreement, but they both knew there would be folks in Elk Tooth's path. That was the way the Cheyenne wanted it.

Taylor's eyes swept the plains. It would seem that across all that vast flatness a man could be seen for miles, but it was all illusion. The plains were cut by deep, sudden gulleys where a hundred Cheyenne could hide unseen until it was too late for the unwary. He sat his horse without moving until the burial detail had returned. Then they formed up again and swung north and west, the cold wind in their faces.

Windy drifted over beside Taylor and asked, "What the hell do you suppose that is?"

Taylor shifted in his saddle to squint back into the sun. He saw them now too, but couldn't quite make them out, even with his field glasses.

"Wagon train. Seems they got some stock."

"Want to swing back?" Mandalian asked.

"No. They're heading into Outpost Nine, looks like. They'll get the word there, if they haven't already. Most likely they've heard that Mr. Lo is kicking up and have decided to shelter up at Outpost Nine."

Windy nodded. Taylor was undoubtedly right. There was something funny about that wagon train, though. Windy gave it one last hard look, then, having no luck, he shrugged and swung northeast, taking the point as they tracked over Elk Tooth's path.

Taylor had made the right decision. Swinging back to check on that wagon train probably would have cost him some men. Not to combat, however.

That wagon train was a special one, an incongruity rolling across the country that had been stained with the blood of Custer's men not a year earlier. It was big, colorful, bizarre. The wagons were bright, festooned, illustrated. Their stock, shambling along behind the wagons, or locked in cages, was most unusual.

Grimaldi's Spectacular Continental Circus rolled through Wyoming, and Taylor's boys would have found that fascinating. What would have been irresistible to the Easy Company forces, however, were the three young ladies who sat on the tailgate of the last wagon, dressed only in their chemises, which they had hiked up well above the knees at the urging of a warm sun.

Six feminine, nicely turned, and firmly fleshed legs flashed in the sunlight as the Grimaldi Circus rolled and lurched across the High Plains.

The girl in the middle was long-legged, with full, pouting lips and a lot of rich dark hair that tumbled free in the sunlight just now. She had those slashing, dark eyes that warned of a temper, and a tempting, full-breasted figure that caused such warnings to be ignored by men. This was Carla Bramante, palm reader, veil dancer, hellion.

She was flanked by two identical blonds: Ava and Anna Boles, twin sisters, magician's assistants, sideshow team. They each possessed the same lush figure. Perhaps they could now look back and see their prime, but it wasn't far behind. Their mouths were small and dabbed with red. They had flawless white skin that flowed evenly across their dumpling breasts, down across their wide, vigorous-looking hips and slightly full thighs.

Ahead of this wagon rolled three cage wagons containing a genuine Siberian tiger, a tired, ancient African lion, and a black bear. Beside and between the wagons, three camels plodded along, their rubbery, outsized lips flecked with foam. There were seven beautiful white geldings, three chimpanzees, and a nine-year-old female Indian elephant named Jumbo, gender and originality aside.

There were probably half a hundred elephants named Jumbo working in circuses in America. With the publicity the original had gotten as the largest animal walking the earth, the name drew them in. Originality be damned; it was those ticket sales that mattered to old man Grimaldi.

They rumbled on, the wagons listing and screeching. The

17

animals lifted their weary heads from time to time, sniffing for water while the men watched the horizon, wary of Indians. Mostly they stumbled on, one foot before the next. The prairie had that way about it. It smothered a man, strapping the senses, blinding thought with stultifying sameness.

But that was not the case with Arturo Mercator.

Grimaldi's wagon went first, followed by the tiger cage. Behind these were the various living-quarters wagons, then the lion and bear, the spurious Jumbo, and finally the wagon that carried Carla and the Boles twins.

Yet that was not the very tail of the party. Behind the last wagon marched Arturo Mercator, pleading, cursing, threatening.

He was not blinded by the prairie, but by the face and form of Carla.

"Please. Put down your skirt! Such a shame. I'm afraid the men will see you. Have you no decency?"

Carla tossed her head and looked out across the grasslands, disdaining reply.

"I'm sorry," Arturo shouted. "I thought he was putting hands all over you. I went crazy. I'm sorry I stuck him with my knife."

Carla whispered something to Anna Boles, who began giggling hysterically. She lifted her legs, holding her chemise just above her knees, and turned them, looking at them. It was enough to drive Arturo to the edge of madness.

"I love you. Marry me!" The wagon hit a rut and lurched, bouncing the three women into the air a few inches. "I'll tame my temper for you, Carla!"

Then, since he wasn't looking where he walked, but only at the long limbs, the sun-bright hair and limpid eyes of Carla Bramante, Arturo hit a fresh, warm elephant turd with his foot and sank to his ankle.

Arturo cursed, Carla laughed, and the wagon rolled on.

Milo Grimaldi was not laughing or smiling, or even managing a decent deadpan. The sweat dribbled down his coarse face, the sun was hot on the back of his hands. The wind was cold, and the seat of his wagon was blistering his butt.

18

Mrs. Grimaldi sat beside him. The missus had been bitching for the last fifty miles, but finally the prairie had worn even her sharp tongue to a blunt edge.

"You'd think there had to be a town. Something. What kind of a place is this?" Milo grumbled to himself, repeating his befuddlement endlessly, as if in some way that chanted repetition could banish the prairie.

"Why did we leave the railroad?" he asked himself. The missus had formerly jumped in here with both feet. Now she was exhausted, and Milo had to perform both parts himself.

"Sure, we do a little damage, and the money runs out. With no hay for the animals, we have no choice but to detrain. All this grass." He waved a hand. "All free."

Someone had told Milo that Montana was booming, with the mines in full gear, the miners ready to throw their gold at anything resembling a woman, at any entertainment after months in the cold, empty hills.

But Milo hadn't really understood how far apart things were in this country. In Europe it was different, settled, civilized.

"When we reach the army fort?"

Milo's head came around. The voice was so small and hoarse, so different from the missus' usual rasping, shutter-rattling voice, that he wasn't sure someone had spoken at first.

She repeated the question. "How far the army fort?"

"Tomorrow we'll be in there," Milo said with a lack of confidence. A passing party of buffalo skinners had told them of Outpost Nine. There they could rest, refill their water barrels and, most importantly, perform. If these American soldiers were anything like those Milo Grimaldi had known in Europe and South America, they were every bit as starved for entertainment and women as those miners in Montana could possibly be.

Milo found that thought momentarily cheering, and he broke into a tuneful whistling. That whistling would have been strangled in his throat if he had glanced toward the low, oak-studded knoll to the north at that moment. There, watching with narrowed eyes and intense interest, was a party of mounted Cheyenne braves.

19

• • •

The sentry on the south wall saw the dust pluming into the windy skies, to be torn apart and drifted across the prairie. The coach was running hard, and judging by the way the driver sat the box, it was Gus McCrae driving.

The sentry called down, "Coach coming in!"

A runner took the word to the orderly room, and Ben Cohen rose, tapping at the captain's door.

"Coach coming in, sir," the first sergeant said.

Captain Conway stood with a touch of weariness, and crossed to the hat rack, where he put on and carefully positioned his hat before following his sergeant out into the clear, crisp afternoon.

Matt Kincaid had also gotten the word, and was coming toward the flagpole to join them. Flora Conway, in that new blue satin dress, and Maggie Cohen watched from the door of the Conways' quarters.

"You have a recruit on this stage, Ben?" Captain Conway asked.

"Yessir."

"I think it'd be best if you indoctrinate him after I have ushered Mr. DeQueen off parade."

"Yessir."

They waited in edgy silence, watching as the gates were slowly opened and Gus McRae, looking like the devil had chased him up from Cheyenne, rolled that Concord stage into Outpost Number Nine.

The captain, with Kincaid at his shoulder, stood waiting as the dust swirled and settled. That rain had kept the dust down for approximately three hours, no more. Now every movement, every puff of wind, set it to drifting across the parade.

There were a few curious soldiers watching the stage, perhaps hoping for a woman passenger, Wolfgang Holzer and Cutter Grimes among them. Cohen glared at them, but without a direct order they weren't likely to move along.

It was then that the crash of metal against stone and metal against metal sounded from the mess hall, and all heads snapped that way. Conway shot one quick, meaningful glance at Cohen, sending him at a run toward Rothausen's kitchen.

The stage rocked to a stop, swaying on the springs. Cohen dashed past Holzer, grimacing as another bang echoed from the kitchen.

"You!" Ben panted, leveling a finger at Holzer. "Have someone meet the new recruit and read him out. Anybody," Ben said over his shoulder, "just so it's not you!"

Then Cohen was gone and Holzer stood there, touching his chest. Something about a new recruit. His face twisted with puzzlement, then brightened.

Bates DeQueen stepped down from the coach and stood dusting off his hat. A narrow-faced man with dark, thinning hair, he wore a brown twill suit and a brown derby. He lifted his eyes to Captain Conway and Matt Kincaid, who approached him with warm smiles and wary eyes.

"Welcome to Outpost Nine, sir," Captain Conway said. He offered his hand to DeQueen and the newspaperman took it, measuring the man before him. Tall, competent-looking, a Southern gentleman apparently. He had the manner, DeQueen decided.

He was also army through and through. Yet he appeared a trifle old for his grade, and that gave DeQueen pause to wonder. It was early to be making guesses, premature to be judging a man, but Bates DeQueen believed he had a talent for reading character, and he thought himself, if not infallible, to be ninety percent accurate. His instincts had served him well in the past, and he had no reason to doubt they would now.

That instinct was what had made him the reporter he was. After all, we do not live in a world where a man admits to his failings, where the truth is spoken regardless of personal considerations.

"Would you like to come inside, sir? I am sure you have had a long and dry trip."

"I appreciate it. Thanks," DeQueen said.

His eyes narrowed slightly as the two women on the porch came forward to meet them. That taller, elegant lady, woman of breeding with a smile at once genuine and facile. Was she the captain's lady?

21

DeQueen smiled warmly as he was introduced to Flora Conway, who took his hand with genuine welcome. Maggie Cohen, he was told, was the first sergeant's wife. A sturdy Irishwoman with snapping blue eyes and the roses of good health blooming on her cheeks.

The tea was set out for them, and the men went into the captain's quarters, followed by the ladies. Bates DeQueen was weary. Dust clogged his ears, stiffened his hair, and had lightened the color of his dark brown suit by two shades.

Still he was alert, his sharp mind evaluating all he saw and heard. This was a man who never relaxed. Captain Conway saw it and he glanced at Flora, but his wife had already read the same danger signals in DeQueen's dark eyes.

This was a man to be wary of. Most wary.

After DeQueen had stepped down and been escorted to the captain's quarters, the stage driver had handed down the baggage and mail he was carrying, then slowly walked his hot horses toward the paddock area, where he could switch teams.

Only then, as the coach rolled away, did the other disembarking passenger come into Wolfgang Holzer's view. He stood on the far side of the coach, his massive shoulders hunched, his round, open face vaguely amiable.

Big! Jesus!

He was as tall as Stretch Dobbs and as thick as Dutch Rothausen, without the belly. Holzer tightened his belt and strode over towards him. The recruit grew bigger with each step, and Wolfgang swallowed hard as he drew nearer. It was enough to give a man second thoughts, but he had promised Ben Cohen.

Wolfgang Holzer had only half an understanding of Ben Cohen's speech, but he had heard this welcoming ritual repeated so many times that he had it memorized exactly. He therefore stepped in front of Lumpy Torkleson and, with an iron-heavy accent, told the recruit:

"Welcome to Easy Company. If you keep you mout' shut and your ears open, you'll find us firm but fair. If you fuck up, you can give your soul to Jesus, because your ass vill belong to *me*! I am Sergeant Cohen and I am the first soldier."

Torkleson cocked his head like some mammoth, puzzled puppy and gawked at this stiff-spined, gesturing private who announced himself as the first shirt. The guttural welcome went on.

"Ven I say froggy I expect you to jump. If you tink you can vhip me . . ." Wolfie hesitated here. He did know what that part meant and he shuddered as he looked up at the towering recruit before him. "I'll be glad to take off my stripes and show you the error of your vays. If you're ready, soldier, go ofer to the kitchen and tell em I said to coffee and grub you before you report to your squad leader."

"Well, thank you very kindly, Sarge," Lumpy Torkleson said with genuine friendliness. "I could use a bite to eat."

"Vell, tank you," Wolgang answered, clicking his heels. "I could use a bite to eat, too."

"Where is the mess hall?" Lumpy asked, squinting into the brilliant sunlight.

"Vell," Wolfgang Holzer replied, "vhere is the mess hall too."

"Are you funnin' me?"

"Vell, I am funnin' you."

"That's what I thought." Torkleson grinned and thumped Holzer on the chest. "You're a joker, Sarge. Come on, I think my nose has just located that mess hall."

Wolfgang Holzer walked along with Torkleson. Entering the mess hall, they heard one muffled thud and then a sigh. They glanced at each other and peered in through the kitchen door.

Cohen was there, rolling his sleeves down, and Dutch Rothausen was cutting a buffalo steak for the red welt under his eye, which would be a first-rate shiner by morning.

Sergeant Cohen glanced up, ready to chew Wolfie out for entering the kitchen. But there was little point in chewing out Holzer's butt. He simply nodded, cocking his head, as if by listening intently he would come to understand the language.

"Enough" Ben told Rothausen. "And this time I'm not kidding." He waved his hands in a gesture of finality. "No more of this crap."

23

"Ben..." Rothausen was frustrated, angry, lost for words. "I need some help!"

"Nobody can work for you, Dutch!"

Cohen sighed again, and then his eyes settled on the man behind Holzer. An affable-looking hulk of a man. Cohen crooked a finger. "Come here."

"Me?"

"Yes, you, goddamit! You think I'm talking to that Sioux behind you?"

Torkleson turned his head, his eyes puzzled. There was no Indian there. "You were funnin'," he said with a wide grin.

"Jesus God!" Ben Cohen breathed. He wiped his hand across his face. Dutch was leaning against the cutting block, a steak draped over his face. Holzer was nodding, understanding nothing.

"You know who I am, soldier?" Ben Cohen asked, stepping forward.

"No I don't, Sergeant."

"You're the new man, Torkleson?"

"That's right."

"Welcome to Easy Company," Ben Cohen said heavily. "If you keep your mouth shut and your ears open, you'll find us firm but fair. If you fuck up, you can give your soul to Jesus, because your ass will belong to me! I am Sergeant Cohen, and I—"

"Beg pardon," Torkleson interrupted, his face a model of puzzlement, "I thought *he* was Sergeant Cohen." He nodded toward Holzer, who clicked his heels and nodded, and Ben Cohen just gave it up.

"Your squad leader will be Corporal Wojensky. You're temporarily assigned KP. Dutch!"

"What?" Rothausen answered from behind that huge slab of red meat.

"He's yours for now."

"Mmph," Rothausen answered, and Torkleson peeled off his tunic, rolling up his sleeves.

"Holzer," Ben Cohen said, "you may as well stick around and help for a while."

24

"Yes, certainly!" Holzer said. He bowed sharply. Ben Cohen turned then and, shaking his head, walked toward the mess hall door. When he glanced back, Holzer was following him.

three

Bates DeQueen nodded his acceptance of a third cup of coffee and touched the flame of his match to his pipe bowl, sending tendrils of blue-gray smoke into the air, curling toward the low, nearly dry ceiling of the Conways' quarters.

Lieutenant Kincaid leaned against the wall, smoking a cigar. The captain's lady was clearing away the last of the dinner dishes, with help from Maggie Cohen.

"That was a fine meal, I'll say it again, Mrs. Conway," DeQueen commented, patting his stomach with satisfaction.

"Thank you again," Mrs. Conway said with an easy smile. "But part of the credit must go to Maggie. It was her plum pudding, her bread."

"Maggie Cohen is nearly as indispensable to Outpost Nine as her husband is," Captain Conway remarked.

"That would be Master Sergeant Cohen?" DeQueen asked.

"The very same. Don't tell him I said this," the captain said, leaning forward, "but he's the man who keeps the clockwork oiled around here."

"Then you do feel that your fort is run efficiently," DeQueen said with a sharpness Matt Kincaid didn't care for.

"Technically we're not a fort," Matt reminded him.

"I know. Outpost Number Nine," DeQueen said, correcting himself. "But still—you gentlemen both feel that you do run an effective operation."

"We do not operate with as much effectiveness as I would like," Conway said frankly. "But given our circumstances, I believe that we are as effective as possible."

27

DeQueen didn't use a notebook, but Matt could see the reporter mentally copying down every remark.

Flora glanced at Captain Conway and some unseen signal passed between them. The captain's lady said, "If you gentlemen will excuse us, Maggie and I will tend to our dishes. Effectively, I hope," she added devilishly.

Matt suppressed a grin. If he was ever to marry, he only hoped he would be as lucky as Conway had been. She was one of a kind, Flora Conway. She was behind her man all the way, and the captain knew it.

"Let me make my position clear," DeQueen said, rising to move around the room, his pipe trailing smoke. "I am here on a fact-finding mission, Captain. It is difficult for those of us in the East to understand the situation out here. Difficult to understand how an experienced officer like Colonel Custer could have bungled his—"

Matt boiled over at that, and he interrupted. "Little Big Horn was *not* bungled, sir. I have seen some of the 're-porting' in the Eastern papers concerning that battle. Either Custer is glamorized as a gallant patriot or derided as a glory-hungry fool. Neither is accurate."

"The Seventh Cavalry was literally decimated," De-Queen said mildly. This was what he wanted. Let these officers speak unguardedly.

"It was simply a matter of meeting a superior force," Conway put in, glancing at Matt, who understood the un-spoken order to put a lid on it.

Fuming, Matt Kincaid turned his back momentarily.

"That certainly must be an oversimplification," DeQueen went on, a short smile forming around his pipestem.

"It is. When you have the time," Conway volunteered, "I would be happy to reconstruct the entire battle for you as reported by survivors."

"I understood there were none."

"There were many—especially on the winning side," Conway advised him.

"Yes." DeQueen struck another match. His pipe had gone cold. "It is the very possibility of a United States force like the Seventh being destroyed by a band of ragtag Indians that bothers most of our readers. It is inconceivable to most

28

that a nation which has the might to twice defeat the British, and then the Mexicans, should be surprised by the inferior forces of the Sioux Nation."

"There is no mystery about it, sir. Here, we are the inferior force. In numbers, in weapons."

"In weapons!" DeQueen laughed out loud.

"Absolutely," Conway said soberly. "Our weapon of issue is the Springfield Trapdoor .45-70. Many of our enemies are armed with Spencer repeaters. And now and then we run into those damned fifteen-shot Winchester needle guns."

"I was unaware of that. If it is true, and I will check on that, just how can it be?"

"How can it be?" Conway echoed, leaning far forward. He wanted very badly to make this point. "It is a matter of appropriations, sir. I am surprised you haven't heard of this problem already. Custer's troops also carried Springfields, and there was considerable stir about it." He leaned back, explaining, "The Springfield is a converted muzzle-loader. At the end of the Civil War, Ordnance was stuck with thousands of obsolete weapons. Yet Congress did not see fit at that time to rearm the Army of the West. After all, funds are always short, and the end of that conflict brought a reassessment of where the budget should be sliced. It was sliced in armaments."

"Yet the Indian—"

"The Indian, sir. Those at Little Big Horn, those we still fight, are carrying Spencer repeaters issued to them for meat-shooting by the United States Bureau of Indian Affairs!"

"You sound bitter."

"No more so than Custer was at the moment the Indians attacked, I expect," Warner Conway said with ill-concealed rancor.

DeQueen smiled distantly, and Conway realized that he had fallen into the same trap Matt Kincaid had. Well, damn it, it was an emotional issue. Men had died, and more would die because of that bungling.

DeQueen had a way of drawing this bitterness out. Exactly what he did to pry it loose, Conway was not sure, but draw it out he did. DeQueen had taken his seat again in the leather chair, and he nodded slightly with satisfaction.

"At the Indian agencies, one hears quite a different story," DeQueen said, crossing his knees. "Tales of innocent Indians being hunted down and massacred. 'Friendlies,' I believe you call them."

Conway nodded. "I have a force in the field at this moment hunting down a 'friendly' who wintered at the agency, took the new rifles they gave him, and is now out butchering people."

"Sioux?"

"Cheyenne, sir."

"You have witnesses?"

"No, sir," Matt Kincaid interjected softly. "Elk Tooth leaves very few. We just kind of have to go by the type of mutilation we find."

That was meant to jar DeQueen, but he didn't change expressions. "Isn't that all exaggerated, sir? This business of the savage Indian torture. 'Last bullet for the women' and all. Poking around, I have learned that the Indian never tortured or took scalps before the coming of the white man."

"That's simply not true," Warner Conway said. "Warfare has been a way of life with the Plains Indians since time immemorial. The coming of the horse made it an easy way of gaining prestige. As for the scalping, I've seen Indian records a hundred years old illustrated with scenes of torture. I've seen many works of art made from scalps. Squaws sometimes use them to trim their leggings."

"And so we have the noble white man beating back the savage horde." DeQueen knocked the ashes from his pipe and put it in his pocket.

"No, sir. We simply have a war. A very nasty war, as most wars are. And we have internal strife in our own government. The Indian Bureau and the War Department contending with one another. The bureau wants to domesticate the Indian, to set him up with farm tools."

"And the War Department simply wishes to annihilate the red man."

"The War Department simply wishes to protect the settlers in Dakota and in Wyoming while the politicians figure just how they're going to make their peace."

30

"I see." He looked Conway up and down. "But then, you are a career officer."

"May I inquire what you mean by that, sir?" Conway said, holding himself back.

"Nothing." DeQueen shrugged. "But promotions do come faster in time of war, don't they? And it must be a hell of a lot more fun shooting Cheyenne than handing out blankets to the 'friendlies.'"

Conway said nothing. He was afraid to answer just then, afraid of what he might say. DeQueen suddenly rose and said with a yawn, "We must continue this interview another time, I'm afraid. I've had a long journey, and I must turn in."

Flora Conway, still wearing an apron, held DeQueen's hat out to him, and the newspaperman took it, nodding his thanks.

"Matt, will you show our guest to the visiting officers' quarters," Conway said stiffly. Flora glanced at her husband, knowing something was wrong.

"Certainly. Sir?"

Matt gestured with an arm and DeQueen went to the door, Kincaid following him. Warner Conway stood in the center of the room, and as the door closed behind the two men he turned slowly to his wife.

"I never thought a man could get to me like that anymore. But he did. If he weren't here under the aegis of headquarters, I swear—"

"He wants to needle you, Warner," Flora said. "That's the way he goes about his work. You don't have to put up with it. Let Matt show him around."

"Yes. Lucky Matt," Conway said. "I suppose that's best." He put his arms around Flora's waist and smiled, kissing the tip of her nose. "Where's Maggie?"

"She slipped out," Flora said.

"Good. That's the answer I wanted."

"Why?" she asked teasingly. "I thought you liked Maggie."

"I do, woman. It's just that I like you a whole lot more."

She glanced at the closed door. "Is that an invitation?"

"It is."

31

"Good," Flora said, slipping closer to her husband. "That's the answer *I* wanted. Come on. I have ways of releasing your tensions, Captain."

"It sounds quite magical when you put it that way."

"You can call it whatever you want," Flora said. Her hand slid down his thigh and to his crotch, where she cradled his growing erection. She kissed him again, her lips parting, her breathing already quickened. "I feel quite powerful," Flora whispered. "Being the only person on the post who can make the CO come to attention."

"Without even a spoken command," he said. He nuzzled her ear, finding the lobe warm. Touching her throat with his lips, he felt her pulse dancing beneath the smooth white flesh of her throat.

"I'll turn out the lamp," Conway said.

"Why?"

Flora turned and he helped her unbutton her dress. It fell to the floor in a silken whoosh.

"Leave the lamp on low," she whispered. "It's hard to give a proper short-arm inspection in the dark."

Warner hooked his boots off and removed his shirt, watching as Flora undressed in the soft light of the lowered lantern. He liked the soft flow of her shoulders, the sweep and rise of her hips, and as she kicked free of her pantaloons, his eyes focused on the dark, promising triangle between her lithe thighs.

He rose and went to her, feeling her flesh against his. Conways's hands slipped down to her buttocks and he drew her to him. She stood on tiptoes to nudge her pelvis against his.

"I have visions of that damned reporter lurking under our bed," Warner said.

She kissed his chest lightly, then slipped down to let her lips graze his abdomen as Warner let his hand rest on her head.

"He'd have his headline, wouldn't he?" she commented. Flora turned her face up to his, and her eyes were distracted, sensual. "Army captain loves wife."

Her hands searched his cock, and her thumb traced inflaming whorls across the sensitive head of it. She leaned

32

nearer, kissed him, and lifted herself far up on her toes. Flora took the head of his shaft and placed it a bare half-inch inside her warmth, gently stroking up and across her clitoris, driving them both toward a pulsing need.

"We'd better get to that bed," Warner whispered, his mouth going to her throat, chin, breasts in turn.

"Why?" Flora said. Her head lolled on her neck, her voice had become a soft purr. "This is fine. Right here." She eased up a little farther and he felt himself slip easily into her, her warmth encircling him.

"I'm not as young as I was," Warner objected.

"You were never this good when you were young, darling," she murmured, nipping at his shoulder.

Flora lifted a leg, and holding on to his shoulders tightly, she raised the other leg, locking them at the ankles around her husband's waist. She settled with a deeply satisfied sigh onto his full length.

Flora lifted herself slowly, then settled again with a tiny shudder, and bit at Warner's lower lip like a gentle bird feeding.

He could feel her body rearranging itself to perfectly accommodate him; her scent was in his nostrils, rich, pagan, timeless.

"Do you like it?" She nibbled at his throat, touched his ear with her lips, her breath rapid and warm.

"I always like it. This is good." She moved against him as he cradled her ass, spreading her, driving into her. He could feel the fine golden hairs at the base of her spine. "You?" he asked.

"Very good," she slurred. She had gone beyond speech, and her body was only ten thousand bundles of nerves loosely contained by her soft, earthy flesh. She was only sensation, raw and savage. Needlepoints of sensation burst across her pelvis, at her nipples where Warner's mouth teased her, and within, where the pulsing was so intense it seemed to roar through her skull, thrumming in her ears as she swayed, sagged, stiffened, and buried his throbbing erection.

"Don't wait," she told him. "Not this time."

He couldn't have if he'd wanted to. He held her—this

woman, this wife, this pitching and yawing tawny bundle of hot flesh—and he wanted only to sway with her, to ride her, to divide her. He stroked deeply, his legs quivering, arms trembling.

The lantern light glossed her flesh, mottled her face. He saw her distant eyes, the slack jaw, the way her head twisted from side to side as he buried himself in her, and he came undone, climaxing with a trembling vigor.

It was really quite impossible just then to give a damn about the Cheyenne or Bates DeQueen of the *New York Herald*, even for the CO of Outpost Number Nine.

Morning was a different story. The instant of awakening brought a vivid rush of memory to Warner Conway. DeQueen.

He rose, shaved the stubble of beard from his tanned face, and dressed. All the time DeQueen was with him in thought.

The man didn't seem hostile, really, but he was intent on digging up the sensational. Not that Conway doubted DeQueen's intention to be impartial, but the truth is slanted in many ways, often unintentionally.

Reveille sounded sharp and clear just as Captain Conway finished dressing. Flora, in a rose-colored wrapper, brought his coffee to the table. She kissed him and smiled.

"Too old!" she said in contradiction.

"Maybe not last night, Flora. Today I feel it."

"DeQueen?"

He nodded and she said nothing more, sensing that Warner did not want to discuss it any further. Slicing two thick slabs of fresh bread, she toasted them on the iron stove and spread them with the butter that only Pop Evans, of all the inhabitants of the Plains, seemed able to come by.

She rested her chin on her hands and watched as Warner ate, washing down the meal with two cups of black coffee.

Warner realized that he hadn't said three sentences to her, and he apologized. "What have you planned for today, Flora?"

"Besides my dreary monotonous tedium?" she smiled as he did. "Maggie and I are working on that quilt still." Prob-

34

ably it would never be finished. It was something for their hands to be doing while they talked. What would she do without Maggie's company? she often wondered. And it was during those pensive moods that she sometimes felt her heart flutter a little as she thought that a baby might be nice.

"When you talk to Maggie," Conway said, peering over his coffee cup so that his face was screened by the spiral of steam rising from the cup, "how much do you tell her?" He wrestled with his phrasing. "How much? Exactly."

She rose then and walked to him. She wrapped her arms around his neck and pressed her breasts against his back, stirring him.

"Not that much," she whispered. "Our sex is ours. Between us. It is very private and very special between us. I talk about it no more than you would talk to Matt about me. They know it's good with us. They only have to look, dear."

Ben Cohen slammed open the mess hall door, walked to the big blue coffeepot, and poured himself a cup. Then he banged through to the kitchen, calling for Rothausen.

"He's out back, Sarge," Lumpy Torkleson said, peering around the corner. The big man dwarfed the apron he wore, the pot he held in his hand. He looked something like Mama Bear stirring her porridge. "He's chewin' some butt," Lumpy continued. "Didn't like the way the boys was diggin' the garbage pit."

Cohen frowned and commented under his breath, "Probably wasn't big enough." Then his eyes lighted. "Torkleson's the name, ain't it?"

"Yes, Sarge. We met yesterday."

"I was a little busy yesterday. What's that you got there, Torkleson?"

"Just a little oatmeal," Lumpy said with an aw-shucks grin. "Sergeant Rothausen said I could make my own grub as long as I was KP. Truth is, though, I don't think he favors me, Sergeant Cohen."

"He doesn't favor anybody these days." He measured his man and asked, "Can you cook?"

"Me? I cooked to home. Since I was a little tyke. Ma died early."

Cohen edged nearer, putting a hand on Torkleson's arm. "Did you cook breakfast today?"

"No." The aw-shucks smile again. "Sergeant Rothausen says I don't have no experience that counts with him. Says this is his kitchen and for me to keep hands off everything but the pots and pans. Why?" Lumpy's eyes narrowed slightly.

Ben Cohen stepped even nearer. "I want you to whip up a breakfast. A good, hot breakfast. Can you do it?"

"Sergeant Rothausen said—"

"Can you see these stripes, Torkleson?" Ben Cohen said loudly.

"Yes, Sergeant, I can!" Torkleson had come to a sort of attention, porridge pot in hand, wooden spoon at his side.

"I'm ordering you to fix a breakfast, Torkleson. Toast. Coffee." He counted the order out on his thick fingers, and Torkleson's goggle eyes followed his gestures. "Three eggs. Ham. Have you got that, Torkleson?"

"I've got it, Sergeant!"

"Good. Snap to it now, and when it's ready, take it to the visiting officers' quarters and serve it to the civilian, DeQueen."

"Yessir."

"Sergeant," Cohen corrected.

"Yes, Sergeant Cohen."

"And better get a move on," Ben said, glancing toward the door. He himself exited the kitchen before Rothausen could return. He didn't want to face Dutch this time of the morning.

Dutch would rake the big kid over the coals, but at least DeQueen would have a decent breakfast. On his way out the door, Cohen passed Wojensky and Cutter Grimes coming in. Grimes looked like the misery of all creation. Three hundred dollars.

"Stand tall, Grimes," Cohen barked as he walked by him. Grimes straightened, but those shoulders would be fallen again before Cohen was out of sight.

Cohen jotted down a mental note. Talk to Pop Evans. He knew that mercy from that old bandit was a little too much to expect. Still, maybe there was some way to work

36

it off. Ben searched his memory, wondering if he hadn't some leverage he could use on Pop. Nothing came to mind.

The captain's lady had pulled the curtain back, so the old man was on schedule. Cohen hurried his steps a little. He wanted to have coffee boiled in the orderly room before Captain Conway decided to pick up a cup at the mess.

There were some days when he wondered if he wouldn't be better off farming for a living. His reverie was broken as he noticed Wolfgang Holzer walking his horse around the parade, wearing full gear. He started to yell at Holzer to find out what in God's name the man was up to, then realized the futility of it, waved a hand abstractedly, and unlocked the orderly room.

four _____

DeQueen was finishing up the big breakfast the
massive cook's helper had delivered to his quarters when
there was a tap at the door. He dabbed at his mouth with
the linen napkin and called, "Come in."

"Morning, sir," Lieutenant Kincaid said, stepping into
the room, silhouetted briefly by the brilliant backdrop of
the sky. The flag hung limply on the pole. The air was
crisp.

"Yes?" DeQueen said, his eyebrows arching slightly.

"Good morning," Matt said without taking or being offered a seat. "Captain Conway has delegated me to show
you around the post."

"I was hoping the captain himself could see fit to do
that." DeQueen seemed slightly affronted.

"The captain is very busy, as you must realize."

"Yes. Very well. I'll be through in a minute," DeQueen
answered. "But it's not the post I want to see just now. I'm
not here on some sort of barracks inspection, Lieutenant."

"Whatever you wish," Matt answered. "I am at your
disposal. Within certain restrictions."

"Restrictions! I'm damned if I'll be leashed by the army."

"I have strict orders, sir. From headquarters through
Captain Conway. There will be certain restrictions."

"Such as?"

"The obvious, DeQueen. We will not enter hostile territory, nor divulge military secrets. And you will carry a
sidearm."

He held out a spanking-new, blue Colt in an equally
new, flapped holster.

"I hardly think I'll need that," DeQueen said breezily.

39

"I am not a professional soldier. I value human life highly and despise the indiscriminate taking of it."

"So do I, sir," Matt replied softly. "That's why I carry a weapon at all times."

DeQueen sighed audibly, took the pistol as if it were something distasteful, and asked,

Is there anything else?"

"Only that you are not to leave the post unescorted, Mr. DeQueen. It is my responsibility to see that you do not, and I intend to live up to that responsibility."

There was a tension in the air as thick as winter clouds. Matt wanted no part of nursemaiding this greenhorn, and DeQueen was suspicious. Why didn't they want him out on his own? Were they afraid he might find out the truth about this botched, bloody war? Perhaps they simply wanted someone along to hear everything DeQueen himself heard.

"All right," DeQueen agreed disconsolately. "I suppose I have no choice. I know the army and its regulations."

"Then none of this should have surprised you," Matt commented. He tried to soften his stance. "It really is for your own safety and in your own best interests, sir."

"It always is," DeQueen replied sharply. "That's what the mayor of Philadelphia told me up to the moment I finally broke that police corruption ring."

"This isn't Philadelphia, Mr. DeQueen."

"No." There was a heavy silence as DeQueen finished his coffee. Matt stood near the potbellied stove, trying for a smile, an expression that would reflect the positive image headquarters wanted. It wouldn't come.

"Where is it you would like to go, Mr. DeQueen?"

"Where?" DeQueen asked as if the answer were obvious. "I've heard your story, a part of it at least. Now I want to talk to the other side. I want to hear what the Indian has to say. If that can be arranged," he asked with a little smile.

"Of course. We'll ride to the Indian agency this morning."

"Well—" DeQueen started to complain, thought better of it, and said, "That will be a start."

•   •   •

40

The shadows were still long, the air still crisp and cloudless as they rode out onto the plains. It was a long, silent ride, peaceful, with only the creaking of saddle leather, the shuffling sound of the faint breeze in the long grass.

Twice they saw antelope half a mile or so off, and later a small herd of buffalo.

"That's a pitiful sight, isn't it, Lieutenant Kincaid?" DeQueen said. "Four dozen buffalo where there used to be a sea of bison as far as the eye could see. A sea of plenty for the red man. Until we destroyed it."

"That's a small herd," Matt agreed. "But this 'sea of buffalo' you're talking about," he went on. "Just when was that? I've been out West for a time and talked to a good many men who were here in the forties and even the thirties. They never mentioned a 'sea of buffalo.' That's another of those nice-sounding phrases some Eastern writer came up with, and it's been used ever since."

"Don't tell me the buffalo didn't wander this range by the thousands, Lieutenant! Do you take me for a fool?"

"Not at all. I'm just saying you're mistaken. True, buffalo are gregarious creatures, and gather in large herds. And I've seen massive herds myself. Right here at times. But they mow the grass down, sir. And when it's been mowed, they move on. Buffalo are no different than cattle, sir. Only so many can graze to an acre."

"Quite a few less now," DeQueen said.

"True," Matt had to agree. "And it's true an almighty lot of them have been killed for sport, for hides and tongues and little else. Yet it was the changing times that killed the buff off. Before the Indians had rifles, they just plain couldn't kill 'em that easily. It was even harder before they had horses, which haven't been here long, as you know; when those Spanish folks lost some horses and the Indians took to them, that changed the entire way of life on this continent. It made hunting easier. And war."

"But before the white man arrived—"

"Before that, the Indians had other little tricks. Like stampeding them over a bluff, killing hundreds more than they could use. Burning grass started the buffalo to running, as well as everything else that just happened to be there.

41

When you hunt like that, there's terrible waste. And there's no grass left to call the buffalo back to that area ever again. You know," Matt continued, "I was talking once to a professor from Yale, and he estimated that the Indian, 'nature's brother,' had exterminated whole species of Plains animals, by hunting like that. There used to be cougar and black bear. And long before that"—Matt looked around the vast, empty prairie,—"there were trees, all kinds of trees, all burned to ash."

"You're getting far away from my point, sir."

"Am I? I thought I was getting right to it," Matt replied. He kneed his bay to a canter, letting it stretch its legs a little. He had not been trying to lay the blame for the dwindling herds on the Indians, but only to point out that the white buffalo hunters thought no more about the exhaustibility of nature's resources than did those fire-hunting Indians.

They say you only pause to think after it's all gone.

There was a good-sized buffalo wallow still holding water from the brief rain, and Matt let his horse drink as he waited for DeQueen, who was taking it slow and easy, sitting in that saddle was painful, and it probably was. A man had to develop a good set of calluses in all sorts of strange places before those McClellans were comfortable.

Now they began to pass a scattering of patched, worn tipis, with here and there a shack thrown up of discarded lumber, corrugated iron, and brush. The weathered, off-white business office of the Indian agency was still a quarter of a mile off when Tom Weatherby appeared on the porch, peering into the sun to identify the incoming riders.

DeQueen looked around critically, noticing the trading post, the government warehouse, the small green house of Tom Weatherby, the naked and half-naked kids running barefoot behind their horses.

Dust drifted across the hard-packed agency yard, and was picked up by an errant dust devil and swirled off across the prairie.

Tom Weatherby stood, arms crossed, on the agency porch. Three or four Indians peered out as Kincaid and DeQueen stepped down, tying up at the rail. The children squealed around Matt Kincaid, jumping up and down, dark flyaway hair rippling with the movement, dark eyes bright, dirty hands outthrust.

DeQueen watched with curiosity as Matt picked up one tiny, smudge-faced girl who was in danger of being trampled, and moved to his saddlebags. There he withdrew a cheesecloth bundle.

He opened it and handed each kid a square of brown sugar, holding the last piece as the shiny-eyed toddler in his arms took a bite. Then he put the girl down to run off, squealing with delight after the others.

Kincaid noticed DeQueen's eyes on him—appraising, dubious eyes. "A man out here doesn't get to see any kids much. They get to be a little special."

Matt stepped onto the porch, his hand out. The Indian agent took it with two hands, warmly.

"Hello, Matt," Weatherby said. "Bring us a visitor?"

"Yes I did. Tom, this is Bates DeQueen of the *New York Herald* newspaper. Here to look around a little bit. The folks back East are mighty interested in what's going on in the territory just now, it seems."

"Mr. DeQueen."

Tom Weatherby had a genuine smile for DeQueen, as he seemed to have for everyone. A slight, balding man dressed in twill trousers, brown shoes, and rolled-up shirt-sleeves, he put an arm around Kincaid's shoulder and invited both men inside.

Tom Weatherby leaned against the counter that ran through the center of the room, dividing the building into two fairly equal halves. Behind Tom there was a row of shelves containing various merchandise—salt, sugar, tobacco, knives, and pots and pans—crowding against each other. On the far side of the counter were a dozen wooden chairs, a cluttered desk, and a dartboard hanging on the wall, a single dart angling into it.

Three Indians, all Cheyenne, sat in the chairs, glumly studying DeQueen. Their faces were rawhide, seamed with weather and age. Their dark eyes were bright. Two of them wore Hudson's Bay blankets around their shoulders. They were all elderly men. Thinking back, DeQueen realized he had seen no young braves in the compound, despite the numerous children. He asked Tom Weatherby about that.

"They've gone out hunting, most of 'em," the agent said. "True, they could trust us to feed them, but the laying in of stores for the winter is an old habit, and they feel better about having their own meat to eat."

"I want to talk to those Indians," DeQueen said, nodding toward the three Cheyenne across the room.

"I have no objection, if they're of a mind to talk," Tom said. He put a hand on DeQueen's shoulder, a gesture the reporter didn't seem to care for. "Come on over, I'll introduce you, and from there on it's up to you."

The man standing against the wall was called Solitary Tree. In full, it was Solitary Tree Standing on the Sunset Mountain, Tom told him. "That's the reason most Indians have a white man's name to use with us. Pretty as some of their names are, they're a mouthful."

The other two are called Jim Fox and Sun Hawk.

"Mr. DeQueen," Sun Hawk nodded. His English was very good, with only a little of that singsong lilt so common among the Indians. "I have heard of your newspaper. Unfortunately," he apologized, "I get the *Philadelphia Public Ledger* and not the *Herald*."

DeQueen was astonished. He had half expected a series of grunts and pidgin-English phrases. "You should try the *Herald*," DeQueen said, covering his surprise.

"Sun Hawk is an avid reader," Tom said. "As are many Indians now. To know the white man, his policies and his rumors of war, are, after all, quite important. I believe Sitting Bull regularly read both the *Herald* and the *Ledger*."

Sun Hawk nodded his agreement. "I'll leave you alone now," Tom Weatherby said. He returned to where Matt Kincaid waited, and DeQueen got to work.

"How are they treating you here, Sun Hawk?"

"Well enough. For the white man."

"You don't say that with enthusiasm."

Sun Hawk shrugged. "I did not say I was enthusiastic. There are many problems. Now winter is arriving. We have been waiting many months for cattle to arrive. They have not come. Will we have meat for the winter? We do not know."

Jim Fox muttered, "Cow meat is no good for the Indian. Buffalo is what we need. Beef makes sickness."

"We have had infected meat," Sun Hawk explained. "I did not say that right, perhaps." He spread his hands, thinking. "Meat that made us sick. The government buys from the men who will furnish meat most cheaply. Sometimes these men bring bad meat."

"You would like to hunt the buffalo?"

"We would. But who can say where the buffalo are? We cannot ride far. Then the army says we are renegades. Then there is more trouble."

"I see. But some of your young men are out on the plains now, aren't they?"

"Some men. Young men who do not care for the rules."

"*I* do not care for the rules!" Jim Fox said.

DeQueen glanced at Tom Weatherby and asked in a lower voice, "Him? Does he treat you right?"

"Tom is a good man, for a white man. A man who goes by these rules," Sun Hawk said with a shrug. "The rules say no armed bands should leave the agency."

Solitary Tree now spoke for the first time, rapidly, in his native language. Sun Hawk translated.

"Solitary Tree complains that to accept the white man's rule is to live like a dead man, a tethered mustang. He says he was born to roam the plains."

"The army has told me," DeQueen commented, "that they cannot tell the renegade from the friendly Indian on the plains, that the government demands they halt the raids of the renegades, and that the government also demands they respect the rights of the friendlies."

"The same government keeps those who are friendly penned up here and then sends no food," Sun Hawk answered. His voice was mild, but his dark eyes sparked. "If there are some bad Indians, should we all pay?"

"No. You shouldn't. Yet how is the army to read the intention of an armed band? I have heard that there are many who use the buffalo guns the government gives them to kill settlers."

"A very few." Jim Fox shrugged. DeQueen could not read this man's thoughts.

"You see, each man must do what he wishes," Sun Hawk

45

explained. "None of us will be ordered. There is no such Indian law."

"But your great chiefs signed these treaties that promised you would remain near the agency."

"What chiefs?" Jim Fox asked. "I am a chief. Sun Hawk has been a war chief of our tribe. The white man has a funny idea about that, perhaps because his own government is so ordered. With us, a man is elected chief until we no longer care to follow his leadership, and so a treaty cannot be signed. Usually a chief signs only to receive presents from the government. Anyway, there is no way to enforce a chief's command."

"But you"—he looked at Sun Hawk and then at Jim Fox—"you no longer want to fight."

"We do not wish to. We pray we will not have to. But this agency—it promises much, yet little is delivered." Sun Hawk shook his head.

"I will not fight," Jim Fox assured him. "War has changed. When we were young, it was sport. A fast pony, a good bow. Now the cannon have come. To fight now is to lose. There can be no other way."

"How about Elk Tooth?" DeQueen asked, and he saw something change in their expressions. The lines of their lips grew taut, their eyes went cold.

Solitary Tree said something and shrugged.

"What did he say?" DeQueen wanted to know.

"He says Elk Tooth is hunting buffalo. The whites found someone dead and wanted to blame it on Elk Tooth. So now Elk Tooth must run to live."

"These murders, burnings. It is not Elk Tooth," Jim Fox said. "No one has ever seen him do crimes. He is simply blamed because he wishes to ride free with the wind in the long grass. This is something the government—the army— does not want."

DeQueen nodded. Their voices had the ring of truth. Kincaid and Conway themselves had admitted they had no witnesses. It was a story with some pathos in it: a Cheyenne warrior used to roaming the plains, providing for himself, now shackled by the government regulations, driven to hunger by disreputable suppliers. The man had finally, in desperation, left the agency against the rules, and gone on a hunt as his forefathers had from time immemorial.

That had outlawed him, and now every murder or burning, rape or act of plunder was being blamed on Elk Tooth. After all, it wasn't that difficult to make a massacre look to be the work of a Cheyenne, from what Kincaid had said. Every man in the territory knew how to do it—which mutilation to use, which arrow to leave behind.

But DeQueen did not hook himself on that story, although he had risen to the bait. True, false. Some of each? He could read no more in the faces of these agency Indians, but they had given him food for thought.

If that was true about Elk Tooth, then he had a major story. Corruption among the vendors, the beef buyers. Intentional defamation. A war of lies.

Yet the entire truth could not be learned here. DeQueen tamped his pipe, lit it thoughtfully, and said his goodbyes, immersed in thought all the time.

Leaving the building, Matt escorted DeQueen around the reservation. There was little to see. Here and there a poorly tended garden with beans, squash, corn.

"The Indian will never wish to farm," DeQueen said.

"The Indian always did before he had the horse," Matt Kincaid answered. "The Cheyenne drifted down from Minnesota originally. They speak of 'losing the corn' as they came west, meaning they quit tilling the soil with the coming of the horse. But they once were farmers and could be again."

"If they wanted to be. Which they don't," DeQueen snapped.

"That I can't argue with."

The tipis, which required yearly upkeep, were in bad condition. There simply hadn't been that many new hides coming in. The shacks were simply that. Old packing crates, odds and ends of lumber, and found wood. DeQueen reviewed them with disgust.

"It's not much to look at," Matt said, "but you've got to remember, out on the plains in a hard winter, they've lived in the same sort of shelter with less security and with no assurance of finding meat to survive the winter."

"You've got an answer for everything, don't you, Kincaid?"

Matt was thoughtful. "No, sir. I don't have the answers, I'm just trying to put things in perspective. This is a complicated situation here, with government, cultures, and warriors colliding. I don't even know if there is an answer."

"None we'll find here," DeQueen said. "These people have been pretty well tamed, haven't they? Dangerous! That's a joke. They've been degraded and whipped and scorned. This is surely not the enemy, Kincaid."

Matt started to say something, but DeQueen cut him off. "No more of your answers, Lieutenant. I'm here to make up my own mind. And I think I'm starting to get a handle on what's happening out here."

Matt frowned. He wondered just what thoughts DeQueen had picked up from Sun Hawk and the others.

"Who's that?" Bates DeQueen asked, nudging Matt.

Matt turned his head to see a squat, widely built squaw looking at them with huge eyes. A smile split her moon face as Matt looked at her. She was closer to four feet tall than to five, and she had some girth. She wore her dark hair in long braids and was dressed in buckskins. She ducked behind a tipi and Matt shrugged.

They trudged on in silence. Banks of clouds hugged the horizon to the north and the west—high, jumbled clouds that glinted at the upper edges with sunlight gold.

Tom Weatherby was on the porch awaiting their return. He had slipped into a coat with the cooling of the air.

"Seen everything you want to see, Mr. DeQueen?" he inquired.

"There's not much to see, is there?"

"Not really," Weatherby admitted. "But it's tough to get appropriations, tougher to get those appropriation moneys into the right hands. Maybe your article will help," he said hopefully.

Kincaid shook Tom Weatherby's hand and untied his bay, tightening the cinch. They saw her again, standing in the shadows, a short, wide woman with round eyes set in a rounder face.

"Who's that, Tom? What's she want?"

Weatherby glanced that way. "Go home, Quail Song!" he said, shooing her with his hands, and she scurried away, giggling as she ran.

Tom looked at Bates DeQueen, and grinned. "You're a lucky man," the agent said. "Seems maybe Quail Song has chosen you."

"Chosen me?" DeQueen repeated.

"For her husband. Her former husband was taken by the pox. She's getting worried, with winter coming on. She wants a good hunter to bring her plenty of fat buffalo meat."

"Let her get an Indian husband," DeQueeen said. He was in no mood for this, and did not find it humorous or interesting.

"She tried. There's not many unmarried braves around right now. She tried to hook up with a brave named Sand Snake. Followed him everywhere, but he beat her up and chased her home. Now it seems she favors you, Mr. DeQueen. She can tell by your clothes that you are a rich man, a good hunter."

"How absurd," DeQueen grunted, stepping into the saddle. He turned his collar against the wind.

"Not to her. In former times a squaw that didn't have a husband would starve come winter. Quail Song likes to eat; she's scared."

Matt Kincaid was smiling, to Bates DeQueen's disgust. Glancing over his shoulder, DeQueen could see the round, pathetic figure, hands clasped before her, watching back.

Whatever empathy Bates DeQueen felt with the agency Indians, he decided instantly that it did not extend to Quail Song. He turned his horse quickly.

"Let's go, Lieutenant. Quickly, please," he added.

five

The wind rose as Matt Kincaid and Bates DeQueen rode back toward Outpost Number Nine. Overhead the sky was clear, but the horizon was crowded with clouds to the northwest and east.

From time to time, Matt would catch DeQueen looking at him with that odd, appraising glance the newspaperman had. Finally he asked him, "What is it, Mr. DeQueen?"

"I'm not sure I understand you, that's all. Listening to you talk, it seems you only want to shoot, to mow the Indian down. Yet at the agency I noticed you were treated with respect. And you gave those treats to the Indian children back there. Unless that was done only for my benefit."

"It wasn't." Matt looked to the skies, watching as a horsehead-shaped thundercloud slowly rose and was flattened by wind currents aloft. "And you haven't been listening, Mr. DeQueen, if you think I, or Captain Conway, or any of the men at Outpost Nine for that matter, glory in the fighting and killing, or despise the Indian.

"In this complex situation, I live by certain simple rules. An Indian at the agency, by his word, is a friendly. An Indian on the plains is a hostile until he proves otherwise."

"Any Indian!"

"Any Sioux, any Cheyenne, any Arapaho."

"And you would attack on that premise?"

"Of course not. I simply do not presume them to be friendlies. I cannot, sir."

DeQueen said, without a trace of humor, "I would hate

to have you on my jury, Lieutenant Kincaid."

"Or as your judge?"

"That too."

There was still an hour or so of daylight left, and Matt drew up, his bay shifting its feet as he looked at DeQueen. "Feel like making a little detour?"

DeQueen glanced at Kincaid with curiosity. "You want to show me something?"

"That's right."

"Sure," DeQueen agreed.

They dipped down into a dry slough where brown cattails lay broken against the earth, then up along a narrow rill that wound across the grasslands. A single stunted oak grew on a low knoll, and beyond that, as they drew nearer the shadows of the far mountains, they found here and there a blue spruce and one wind-flagged, woodpecker-pocked cedar.

The land suddenly yawned at their feet. A great, hidden chasm opened up. Without slowing his horse, Matt led DeQueen into the wash.

They rode northward in silence, the wind creaking in the brush that grew on the bottom. The bluffs grew higher as they rode, sandy banks that crumbled away with each whim of water and air. A jackrabbit loped away from the approaching horses.

Eventually the wash widened and they came into a teacup of a valley, where some grass grew on an island formed by the forking creek.

A stand of willows circled the island, some gray, dead from hard winters. There were swarms of mosquitoes, bumblebee-sized ones, but all in all it was a pleasant spot, DeQueen decided. Yet there had to be a reason for Kincaid's having brought him here. What was it?

"This is Turkey Creek, DeQueen. Where we stand is Turkey Creed Island. Ring a bell?"

"No." DeQueen searched his memory briefly. "I can't say it does."

"Well, it does to me. Always will."

A crow dipped low, heading toward the willows before it spotted the men and veered off, cawing angrily.

"What is this place?" DeQueen asked, impatient suddenly.

"A burial ground." Matt turned cool eyes on the newspaperman.

"An Indian burial ground?"

"No. One of ours," Matt Kincaid said. "You see, sir, sometimes it is *our* blood. Maybe that never entered into your equation, the figuring up you do when you decide so definitely who is right and who is wrong."

DeQueen seemed somewhat mollified. The wind ran breezy fingers through his dark, thin hair as he wiped his hatband with his scarf.

"I had a full squad," Matt Kincaid said, almost as if he were talking to himself. "Two Delaware scouts, and a cool, clear day for hunting. Three Bears, the Sioux, was the man we were looking for. He had tangled with the Seventh, drifted west, butchered a pair of buffalo hunters—hung one upside down from a tree, they did, cut his belly open, and left him there, holding his guts in his hands."

Matt Kincaid stepped down from his horse, remembering it all in detail, vividly, as he suspected he always would remember it. . . .

Willie Gunn, the Delaware, was chief scout, Sergeant Joe Huggitt his squad leader. Huggitt could have been first sergeant somewhere, but he wanted to stay in the field. The Indians had gotten his wife and young daughter.

Three Bears was vicious, full of white-hate, but they had the numbers on him and the Sioux was running fast, as Willie Gunn pointed out.

"You see?" The Indian pointed out the long poles concealed hurriedly in the brush. "Travois. Three Bears will drag no one, nothing."

He stood, dusting his hands, and Matt asked him, "Where's he heading, Willie?"

"No water. This is a dry year, huh? He will have his horses dead beneath them. I think Dirty Tanks."

"I think he's dead right," Sergeant Huggitt put in. "We know he ain't had water for four days, Lieutenant."

"Dirty Tanks?" Matt hadn't been long in the territory. That was a new one on him.

"It's across Turkey Creek, sir," Huggitt explained. "Not much to see. Two mudholes not much bigger than buffalo wallows. But there's ground seep off the foothills most all year. He's there." Huggitt's eyes lifted to the prairie beyond, and Matt's eyes followed.

"Line the men, Sergeant," Kincaid said. "And I want the men riding loose."

Huggitt stepped back into the saddle, reversing his scarf like a cowboy. He pulled it up over his mouth and nose to protect against the dust. That dust was billowing into the sky, making a marker a half-mile long, hundreds of feet high. They damned sure weren't going to sneak up on Three Bears. But then, the old bastard knew they were coming anyway.

They made night camp a mile west of Turkey Creek, with a double guard posted, no fire after dark. Matt had a cup of dark, bitter coffee in his hand, and he sat sipping it as the smoke from the extinguished fire spiraled into the night sky.

It was still, star-bright. Despite the aura of danger, or maybe because of it, Matt was able to absorb his thoughts totally in the stars, the pale glow of the rising quarter moon, the wind working in the long grass. A low-winging owl was briefly silhouetted against the moon's face.

"Mind if I join you, sir?" Joe Huggitt asked. The big man stood, shirt cuffs rolled up, coffee steaming from the tin cup he held.

"No. Sit down," Matt offered.

He scooted down a ways on the peeled, half-rotted tree trunk he rested on, and Huggitt sat, sighing as he did so.

"This is a hell of a way to make a living, isn't it?"

Huggitt grinned. "I guess it is at that."

"What keeps you at it, Sergeant?"

Huggitt sipped thoughtfully at his coffee. "I've been doing it for a time. I just keep on doing my job, I guess. Too late to start over. I was brought up on a dirt farm in Kansas, sir. Pa, he didn't amount to much, I guess. Hell, he never raised nothing but the bottle, and us boys, we raised hell."

Huggitt was silent, remembering. "But the army gave me some boots, a warm coat, a handsome gun. They fed me good and I slept under a roof that didn't leak most times."

"But you could retire."

"Retirement pay ain't much," he shrugged. "I got nowhere to go. I want to fight Indians, sir," he said honestly, turning his broad, open face toward Matt. "I want to fight 'em, and I want to see 'em die. Because the more I see go down, the better chance there is that I'll have got the ones that got Linda Sue and Missie."

There was a matter-of-factness about Huggitt's statement that chilled Matt Kincaid's spine. He made no response. What was there to say to something like that?

They heard the whoosh of moccasins in the grass and saw the shadowy figure of Willie Gunn coming toward them. Willie stopped before Matt and crouched down, his face bright in the moonlight.

"Men on foot coming toward us," Gunn said, pointing. "Three, maybe four. I think Indian, but not Sioux."

Matt was on his feet in a moment, looking off in the direction the Delaware indicated, but he could see nothing, hear nothing.

"Pass the word, Sergeant. Pass it quietly."

"Who do you think, Willie?" Matt asked him as Huggitt darted away toward his sleeping squad.

"I don't know. I think friendlies, from the way they move. Striding long, not rushing. Too loud."

Matt heard a horse nicker, and then another. They smelled the Indians now. From the corner of his eye he saw his men rising, spreading out, some carrying their boots as they moved. No one wanted to get caught in his bed.

Matt eased into the scattered timber, Joe Huggitt at his side. They watched the moon shadows, the clouds drifting before the moon. There was a soft owl hoot and then the very definite sound of a twig cracking underfoot somewhere not far off.

Matt drew his sidearm, curled his thumb around the hammer, and drew it back, the double click sounding loud in the night. Whoever they were, they were coming in.

They stood pressed against the trees. Glancing over his shoulder, Matt could see the glint of the moon on the rifle barrels of a half-dozen men prone in a shallow gulley.

He found himself staring at one particular spot, afraid to blink. He was surprised to find his muscles knotted with strain. Matt breathed deeply, shaking it off. His eyes swept the empty prairie, examining each shadow, each low, formless mass.

They were not there.

And suddenly they were, as if rising out of the earth. Three men walking widely spaced, striding calmly toward their position. Huggitt's rifle went to his shoulder, and he held his bead on a man's chest as they continued forward.

Matt looked beyond these three, and then to either side, but he saw no others. He let them come within fifty feet before he challenged them.

"Halt! Identify yourselves."

He could see no weapons in their hands, but he was taking no chances. He raised his hand and heard the responding sequence of rapid clicks behind him as his men cocked their Springfields.

There was a moment of silence, then a high-pitched voice answered.

"We are friendly. I am Charmed Wolf."

"What tribe?"

There was a moment of hushed conference. Then, "Cheyenne, but friendly. We wish an escort to Outpost Nine."

Matt glanced at Huggitt, who could only shrug. Gunn could do no more. "Ask them in," the Delaware suggested. "But keep your weapons at the ready."

"Come ahead," Matt called out, and they came toward him, their moccasins whispering across the dew-wet grass.

There were three of the Cheyenne, Charmed Wolf and two old men. They had no weapons, but Huggitt insisted on searching them, and Matt let him do it after he had explained, "Had one count coup on us back on the North Platte by whipping out a hatchet and burying it in Major Haskell's skull."

Matt invited the three Cheyenne to sit by the dead fire. He himself remained standing. "Why have you come here?" he asked.

"It is very bad. Three Bears rides our land. His men were hungry and they attacked our camp. Many men dead, our women carried off. Our horses are taken. He is gone now—"

"Which way?" Willie Gunn interrupted.

"There." Charmed Wolf lifted a finger. "To Dirty Tanks, I think. We are camped on Turkey Creek, and it is dry. They wanted water for their horses. I think when he found none, Three Bears punished us for his ill luck."

Matt frowned. Studying the Cheyenne, he believed them. Charmed Wolf looked haggard, his face drawn. The two old men seemed ready to drop.

"Many of us are dead. We have no horses, now we cannot hunt. Three Bears may come back and kill us. Take us to the outpost so we may pitch our tents nearby."

"I can't. Not just now. We ride after Three Bears. We will find him and then you will have no reason to worry."

"We will still have no food, no horses."

One of the old men said, in a voice cracked and dry, "When I lay down my gun, white man promised me meat." He signed "meat" with his expressive, gnarled hands. "And safety. The man who promised is gone back to Washington. Who will honor his promise?"

Matt inhaled sharply. There were too many men from Washington making promises and then going back home. He studied the seamed face of the old man.

"I can't take you back to Outpost Nine now."

"Can you spare rifles to protect us?"

"No."

"Food for our women and babies?"

Matt shook his head again. The dark eyes pleaded with him. What could he offer them? "Can't you walk?"

"We have many wounded. Many. No food."

Matt looked to his squad leader. "What do you think, Joe?"

"There's no solution. Maybe we could detour by their camp, split out some rations, see if we can help with the doctoring. Besides that—" he shrugged.

"But can we trust them?"

"That's a decision on your shoulders, Lieutenant."

It could be that the Cheyenne were lying. It could also be that to ignore their plea for help would doom their old, their women, their children. It came down to the kind of man Matt Kincaid was. Was he the kind to turn his back on them? There were times when a man had to go on faith alone, his basic sense of decency, right and wrong.

The Cheyennes' camp was on their way to Dirty Tanks. There was a chance of making allies of former enemies here. There were folks who needed help.

"All right," Matt decided. "We will return with you to your camp. We can give you food and bandages. After we have finished with Three Bears, we will return and escort you to Outpost Nine."

It was settled, then. They would ride out at dawn. "But ride loose," Matt told Huggitt. "I think they're all right, but it's best to be ready."

The Cheyenne slept in the middle of the camp, a guard posted near them. With the dawn, they were out onto the chill plains, following the three friendlies back toward their ravaged camp on Turkey Creek.

Matt, who didn't yet know the country well, was surprised at the huge gap in the earth that opened up suddenly before them. Smoke rose from a single fire. Seven or eight tipis were pitched on a sandy island below. He could see children and women in the camp, and that reassured him somewhat.

Still, it was a bad place to have a force caught, between those high-rising sandy bluffs, and so he split his men, leaving a dozen behind to sit sentry.

Then they followed the Cheyenne down the slope and into their camp.

They heard the sounds of men in pain, saw a recently dead man lying on the ground, awaiting burial, saw the dirty children running away in fright as Matt's force approached.

Matt swung down, walked to a tipi, and glanced inside. A wounded man sat there holding the stump of an arm. He had a filthy rag wrapped around it. Lifting the rag, Matt was driven back by the terrible stench of gangrene.

He went back out, taking gasping breaths of the cold, clean air. Willie Gunn, who had circled the island, searching the heavy stands of willow, rode up, shaking his head.

"They have no horses, Lieutenant."

"I haven't seen a gun, either, sir," Huggitt said. "But

they're in almighty poor shape here. Had a nursing squaw follow me, begging me for water."

Matt looked at his sergeant, wondering.

"I gave her one of my canteens," Huggitt shrugged, appearing sheepish as his role of Indian-hater was punctured.

"Let's see what we can do, then. We'll be hitting Dirty Tanks tomorrow. Will there be water left for us, Willie?"

"I think so, unless Three Bears poisons it, and an Indian almost never does that. He never knows when he might need the Tanks again himself."

"That's what I was thinking," Matt said. "Find an *olla*, or whatever they call their pots. Have each man dump half his canteen into it for these people. As for the rations, make it whatever a man feels he can spare."

"Some will give nothing."

"All right. I won't make it an order. I can't." Matt turned back toward the village. "Now let's see if we can't patch up a few of these wounded folks. Joe, you're handy with the meat-stiching, aren't you?"

"I've done it a time or two. But never on no damned Cheyenne."

Nevertheless, he swung down and rummaged in his saddlebags for his medical supplies. Matt glanced toward his sentries, spread out along the bluff. Corporal Travis lifted a hand in response. All clear.

Matt got to work on the injured, bandaging a chest wound on an old man, resplinting a leg. As he worked, he kept his eyes open, but he saw no rifles in this camp, and the sentries saw no sign of the Sioux.

There was plenty of stitching and bandaging. Two or three men with bad wounds were beyond help. Matt gave them morphine to ease the pain and water to quench their demanding thirst.

When he had finished with the last of them, he came out of the tipi to find the shadows crawling into the canyon. Sunset was a deep orange above the dark silhouettes of the far mountains. He surprised Joe Huggitt playing ball with a small, skinny Cheyenne boy.

Joe flushed with embarrassment. He tossed the ball in his palm and said to Matt, "Hell, I'd play with Three Bears' kids, I reckon. These kids, they didn't make the world, they got nothin' to do with what the old folks screwed up."

He went on, "I used to play with my little girl, Lieutenant. Every chance I got. You know, they ain't little for long. They grow up, get to be like us, and we encourage it as if we were in good shape, you know? Hell, these are the best people you'll ever meet, these pint-sized ones."

It was peaceful at that hour. Homeward-bound flocks of doves cut silhouettes against the sundown sky. Charmed Wolf came up to Kincaid again and again to thank him, and he was not the only one.

Several of the Cheyenne had given gifts to the soldiers. Beads were draped around the necks of several of Matt's men. Some had feathers poked into their hatbands. Matt let the regulations go a bit slack for the time being. His men had been drawn as taut as new wire.

The shadows had filled the gulley now, and the Cheyenne had started a fire. Matt glanced at it uneasily, but said nothing. He sent out a party to relieve his sentries.

They sat around the fire with the Cheyenne as dusk settled, sharing an evening meal while the fire blazed. Night camp, he decided, could not be in this wash. In fact, it caused him to wonder why the Cheyenne had chosen this spot. Perhaps they figured any place invisible from the flats was safe.

He thought of asking Charmed Wolf, but he didn't see the man around. Matt stood and searched the camp, and it was then that it hit him.

"Huggitt," he said conversationally, "the women and kids, where are they?"

Huggitt looked around casually, his dark face drawn down into a heavy scowl.

"Maybe they're all inside the tipis," Huggitt suggested hopefully.

"Maybe. Maybe we ought to pull out, Hugg."

"I think so." Carefully, Huggitt placed his tin cup down and rose, stretching his arms. He nodded to the Cheyenne who were sitting around them, and he slowly filtered away, touching a man here and there on the shoulder.

I'm getting jumpy, Matt told himself. Still, it would be

a good idea to pull out. He'd feel better once they had their night camp on high ground.

He didn't plan on saying anything to the Cheyenne. Just rise, pull back, and get the hell out of that gulley.

Why was he mistrustful now? Matt knew the Cheyenne had been hit hard. They didn't fake those wounds or inflict them on themselves.

I'm getting damned jumpy.

"Stay here with us," Charmed Wolf said with an expansive gesture. "We will talk a time longer, exchange information."

Matt shook his head slightly. Off to the north he saw Huggitt leading both their horses toward them. And in the willows to the west a shadowy movement. A glint of moonlight. Behind a tipi, then, Matt saw a Cheyenne with a rifle, and he shoved Charmed Wolf aside and drew his Scoff as he shouted to Huggitt.

"Get 'em out of here, Hugg!"

Huggitt's head snapped around, and a fraction of a second later the roar of a shot registered in Matt Kincaid's brain. Huggitt's jaw was torn off by the shot, his shirt was a wash of blood.

Charmed Wolf had been knocked to the ground, and now Matt saw the Cheyenne's hand fill with a pistol he had hidden somewhere. Matt turned and triggered two shots, the powder smoke filling the space between them so that Matt could hardly see Charmed Wolf.

He didn't have to see him to know he was dead. The wolf had lost his charm.

There was a fusillade of gunfire from the willows, and Matt saw one of his men go down, saw an army pony racing free, dragging a man.

The Cheyenne all had weapons now, guns concealed beneath their blankets or in their tipis, and Matt moved through a hail of fire. He shot one brave, and saw him tumble back into the roaring fire—the signal fire—as a war party of Sioux joined the fight, charging up the gulley from the south.

He tried to form his men, tried to shout commands, but it was chaos, every man for himself, and the Cheyenne and

61

Sioux forces had them in a crossfire.

Matt wondered what had happened to his sentries. Likely they had been lulled by the seeming goodwill of the Cheyenne, the report that Three Bears was running hard to the west.

There was no time to ponder it just then. Matt raced toward his horse and saw it dance away, frightened by the gunfire, and grabbed up the reins to Huggitt's war-trained horse instead.

He drove hard for the dry creek, firing across his shoulder as he rode. Already he could see that they had been cut to ribbons. A soldier reared up out of the brush and Matt grabbed his hand, trying to yank him up onto the cantle behind him.

But an Indian bullet tagged the soldier in the throat, and Matt felt his hand squeeze hard once before he went limp and fell dead to the sandy earth.

He had still worn a necklace of beads around his neck.

A sudden flash of pain exploded in Matt's upper back and he was nearly slammed from the saddle. He managed to hang on as the horse ran on wildly. The world spun and filled with fire. Matt grabbed for the reins as the horse charged on. He only wanted to break out, to re-form the men, to take the battle to Three Bears.

But already he knew it was useless. His men lay broken, bloodied, and battered on Turkey Creek Island.

"Six of us survived," Matt Kincaid told Bates DeQueen as twilight shadowed Turkey Creek Island. "There was an inquiry, and they found no fault with me. But I could not judge myself so lightly.

"Those men, good men, died because of me. Because I was a little green, a little too trusting. I've dreamed about it many a night," he said. "And thought about it many waking hours. You see, DeQueen, what I had forgotten was that this is a war! Maybe there just isn't room for humanitarianism. Not if you want to get out of here alive."

"And so you follow that rule," DeQueen said. They heeled their horses forward, Matt leading the reporter toward a place where the bluffs had crumbled down into the creek.

"That's right. An agency Indian is a friendly. Any Indian on the plains is a hostile until he proves otherwise."

DeQueen thought of something. "But the wounds those Cheyenne had suffered..."

Matt turned his head toward him. The sky was purpling, the horses moving easily. "They had picked them up raiding a settlement two days before. They'd killed five men and a woman there."

"And Three Bears?"

"Three Bears no longer rides the plains," Matt told him. "He was cut down at Washoe."

But his ghost still rode the prairie, and would as long as Matt Kincaid lived.

It was nearly dark when they came within sight of Outpost Number Nine. The two men had ridden silently, each sorting out his own thoughts.

There was smoke rising from the mess hall chimney already. Beyond the deadline, the "blanket Indians" had their cookfires going. But there was something else quite startling.

Matt stood in his stirrups. "What the hell is that?"

DeQueen looked that way as well, and even his usually expressionless face was bracketed with curiosity. It was difficult to tell, but as they drew nearer, Matt could make out the wagons, the unique stock being driven among them, and he whistled.

"I'll be damned if it isn't a circus."

"Looks like one, doesn't it?" DeQueen said.

"There's something else, DeQueen," Matt told him. "I guess she gained ground on us while we sat at Turkey Creek."

DeQueen was puzzled, and Matt turned in the saddle, nodding at the squat, pathetic figure of Quail Song, who stood a hundred yards behind them, a sack of some kind over her shoulder.

DeQueen scowled and heeled his horse forward. They hurried on toward Outpost Nine.

63

six

Captain Conway's head came up at the sound of Sergeant Ben Cohen's familiar knock. The first sergeant came in and reported, "A civilian here to see you, sir."

"Not a newspaper reporter?" Conway asked with a hint of a smile. Ben smiled back.

"No, sir. I don't think you'll hardly believe this one."

Conway frowned and, failing to decipher Ben's meaning, said, "Ask the gentleman in, Ben."

Cohen turned and went out, and in a moment the civilian appeared. He wore a handlebar mustache, waxed to a dark gloss, a top hat, and a dark coat with a scarlet lining. A gold watch chain was draped across his vest. Warner Conway stood, offering his hand.

"Sit down, sir," the captain said.

"Thank you. Very much," the civilian replied, and Conway heard the strong Middle European accent in those few words.

"How can I be of assistance to you?" Conway asked.

"Milo Grimaldi," the civilian introduced himself. "You may have heard the name."

Conway shook his head. "Sorry."

"No?" Grimaldi's chest puffed out a little as he said, "We played three performances in Washington City. At one, the President was in attendance." Milo hedged, "Of course, this was some time back."

"You are a performer?"

"A showman," Milo said grandly. "The owner, director, and ringmaster of Grimaldi's Spectacular Continental Circus."

"A circus? And you are separated from your show?" Conway asked.

"Separated! No, sir. We are here. Grimaldi has arrived!" Milo Grimaldi said with a grand gesture.

"Across the plains!"

"Certainly."

"Are all your people all right?" Conway asked with concern.

"But of course. Why not?"

"Haven't you heard of the hostilities?"

"Hostilities?" Milo was uncertain. "Oh, with the Indians. Yes." He nodded. "But I have met many Indians. Always very nice. Silent and aloof. But very nice always to me."

"Then you haven't met some of our Indians, Mr. Grimaldi."

"Ah, this is what some people warned me. But we saw no Indians, sir. May I explain now my business?" He hunched forward in his chair, dark eyes thoughtful. He concentrated, sucking at his lower lip.

"Go ahead," Conway encouraged.

"We are on our way to Montana. But our stores are very low, our water nearly gone."

"I cannot offer you an escort at this time," Captain Conway hastened to point out. Grimaldi waved his hands.

"No, no, this is not my request. We merely wish to share your water and be permitted to set up our camp. We wish to perform, sir, to earn a few dollars to see us through to Montana."

Conway's eyebrows rose. "Here?" he asked dubiously.

"I am sure your men would find it most entertaining, Captain."

"I'm sure they would too," Conway said. "You will have a midway set up?"

"Of course!"

Conway nodded thoughtfully. "I really have no substantial objection, Mr. Grimaldi. As you say, the men would enjoy it. God knows, they deserve some relaxation. As long as the midway games are run honestly."

Grimaldi looked offended. "But of course, sir. I assure

66

you my people are, every one, as honest as Milo Grimaldi himself."

Conway suppressed a smile as he considered that. But these people needed water and sanctuary. That was all right. He would have to caution Ben Cohen to be sure to remind the boys to watch themselves. A thought came to Conway. "You have women with your show?"

"Of course, sir." Grimaldi smiled. "Ah! Not of *that* kind, sir. All my girls are performers. Virgins from Europe."

That would be an attraction worth paying to see, Conway thought wryly.

He stood. "All right, Mr. Grimaldi. I have no objections. If you have questions as to where to draw your water or how to obtain stores, the sergeant at the desk out front will be happy to provide you with any help he can along those lines."

Grimaldi thanked the commanding officer and went out, selecting a properly racy angle for his top hat. The orderly room was crowded with soldiers. Odd, it had been empty when Grimaldi came in.

Then he realized why the men were pressing around Ben Cohen and he smiled, waving to the men as he strode out.

Cohen was definitely not smiling. Reb was first in line, but he was being shoved forward by a dozen others. Holzer was waving his hat, and Stretch's head bobbed above everyone else's like a buoy on the tide. Ben was trying to keep things under control quietly, since the captain was in his office, but finally McBride was shoved forward and Ben's inkwell went over on his desk.

He sat stone-still a moment, watching the black rivulet ruin his duty roster. Then he stood like an avenging angel and boomed out, "Goddammit, this is still a military post, and I am still your first soldier! There will be silence! There will be order! I'll give you thirty seconds to clear this orderly room! Any man who isn't outside in a neat file, ready to report by the book, will A, receive no pass for any reason whatsoever, and B, get his ass kicked all the way across the parade!"

Conway heard the tramping of feet and he looked up,

irritated and amused at once. "Any problem out there, Sergeant?" he asked.

"No, sir!"

Conway turned back to his dispatches, knowing that the men had spotted that circus, and any piece of feminine fluff it happened to be carrying, the minute it broke the horizon. It was a little too much to expect that the word wouldn't spread like wildfire and stir some of those long-dormant loins.

Reb McBride tapped twice on the door frame, entered as he was summoned, and snapped to attention before Ben Cohen.

"Corporal McBride requesting a pass off post, Sergeant."

Ben let him stand and stew for a good five minutes as his own temper cooled and he mopped up the ink. "How many men out there, Reb?"

"Everyone who ain't nailed down, Sarge."

"I guess Rothausen will be having plenty of KP help, then. You know better than to bust in here like that."

"Yes, Sergeant, I do!" Reb answered sharply.

"Then why in God's name did you? Chrissakes, McBride, you're supposed to be a corporal."

"Yes, Sergeant. But intelligence reported an unusual sighting. People arriving in flashy wagons. These people, Sergeant, wore long silk clothes. Dresses, I think they call 'em. And they had these bumps on them in odd places. Two like this on the chest, and it caused me to rush to the sergeant to report. The other men wished to be standing by in case there was an order from the sergeant to disperse these strange creatures."

Ben signed a pass, slapped it on the desk, and shook his head. "I just hope every man in that line isn't so full of shit."

"Thank you, Sergeant Cohen." McBride did a tight about-face, winked, and walked out, waving the pass in the air, his hat tilted down over his eyes.

Milo Grimaldi walked through the main gate of Outpost Number Nine, passing the arriving young lieutenant and a pinched-faced civilian. Grimaldi was whistling as he walked, hands thrust deep into his pockets.

He saw Carla Bramante and one of the Boles twins starting a cooking fire, and he called jubilantly to them, "Don't cook! No cooking now. Show tonight! There's a show tonight, get the tents up!"

There was a flurry of activity following that, a bustle, a storming rush, a cacophony of voices shouting directions as the circus people swung to it. Every hand was needed, the women too. The tents were rolled out, staked, and poled, with Jumbo straining on the taut line to run the bulk of the big tent up the center pole.

The sideshows were erected in a little less time. Tents with a framework of lumber, they were assembled by hands that had done this a hundred times before, thrown up, decorated with bunting and fluttering pennants, now and then toppling as someone got too eager. The calliope had been offloaded from the number-three wagon, and now Professor Tillit set his nimble fingers to work, picking out marches and waltzes as the circus rose against the evening sky.

From atop the walls of Outpost Nine, it all seemed a little magical, rising like a tent city on the plains, colorful, musical, rife with hidden delights.

Those who had been able to garner a pass, and that was half of the personnel, busied themselves shining their boots, slicking back their hair, shaving, and splashing their faces with borrowed bay rum, on the chance they would meet a real, breathing, warm woman.

Here and there was a man who did not get excited over the prospect, Cutter Grimes among them. The West Virginian sat dismally on his bunk, eyeing the others. Reb, smelling like a drugstore, barbershop, and ladies' social combined, tried to cheer Cutter.

"Come on, son. Up and at 'em."

"Hell, I ain't gonna go, Reb. What for?" he asked morosely.

"What for? When the hell you think you're going to see another circus, Cutter? They don't come through every five years."

"I got no money," Cutter said. "You ought to know that, Reb."

"I'll lend you some."

Cutter smiled thinly. "I ain't much of a risk. Ask Pop Evans."

"That ain't the same, friend. We're partners. I'll help you, just ask." Reb sat beside Grimes. "There's *women* with that circus, boy. *Women.*"

"I'm engaged to be married," Cutter said.

"That ain't the same as *being* married," Reb said, slapping Cutter's shoulder affectionately. "Come on with me, get your mind off Pop Evans and all for a while."

Cutter was reluctant, but he agreed after much prodding and wheedling. His heart wasn't in it, that was obvious, but he reluctantly rose and halfheartedly shaved.

There was a second man on post who not only didn't have the urge, but knew nothing about the circus's arrival. The word hadn't filtered through to the kitchen, where Lumpy Torkleson scrubbed endlessly on the pots and pans of Dutch Rothausen. Some he had scrubbed twice, some three times.

"I'll teach you to mess around in my kitchen when I'm out," Dutch said for the fortieth time. The cook leaned against the wall, arms folded on his massive chest.

"But, Sarge, Sergeant Cohen told me—"

"And he knows better too!" Dutch said, jabbing at Lumpy with a finger. "Goddammit, Dutch Rothausen's kitchen is his kingdom, and any half-assed recruit or blustering NCO who comes in here trying to change things around is going to pay."

"It was just one breakfast—"

"You can get that copper shinier than that! Just one breakfast today. What about tomorrow? I'll have KPs running my kitchen!"

"I really didn't mean nothin'," Lumpy tried to explain. "I was just following orders."

"Good! Keep following them. Scrub! That's an order, Torkleson."

Lumpy just nodded, sighed, and got back to it. There was nothing else to do. He had walked into the middle of something and now he was stuck.

There was another man in the room now, Lumpy suddenly realized. He lifted his eyes to the corporal standing near the door.

"What the hell is it, Wojensky?" Dutch barked.

"Is that my new man?" the corporal asked.

"He's in your squad, Cohen says."

"His duffel is still out here, Rothausen. He hasn't even been to the barracks yet. Don't you think it's time you released him?"

"Cohen put him on temporary assignment here. By the way, it's still *Sergeant* Rothausen."

"Aw, come on, Dutch," Wojensky grumbled. "What about my man, *Sergeant* Rothausen?"

"When he's through here," Dutch repeated, enjoying his own obstinacy.

"You know, *Sergeant* Rothausen, you're getting to be a pain in the ass," Wojensky said cheerfully. "You've got a wagonload of spuds out front, by the way."

"The hell you say! Where the hell's the teamster? He never said a word." Dutch beamed. "Fresh, real spuds!"

"Just parked that wagon and took off to the circus," said Wojensky.

"Circus?" Dutch's eyes narrowed suspiciously. "What's the gag?"

"No gag. We've got us a real fuckin' circus right outside the gate."

Dutch shook his head as if that idea were too remote to be considered. Then he tapped Lumpy on the shoulder. "Let's get them taters in, KP."

Over the dark line the outpost's wall cut against the evening sky, Dutch saw a yellow pennant waving, and he could hear the music drifting through the night. He looked at Wojensky. "I thought you were ribbing me."

Stretch Dobbs, Holzer, and Malone were drifting up the porch, and Dutch was astonished to see Stretch's flyaway hair slicked down. Malone even looked half sober. The three men stood beside their squad leader, and Stretch said, "Thought we'd head on over now. You coming, Wojensky?"

"In a minute. I'm playing Abe Lincoln, trying to free the slaves. This is Lumpy Torkleson, boys," he said, nodding

71

at the amiable, hulking man with the sack of potatoes over his shoulder. "He'll be in our squad if I can ever get Dut—Sergeant Rothausen to release him from KP."

"Howdy, Torkleson," Malone said, stepping forward, thrusting out a broken-knuckled hand. "I'm Malone." He glanced at his sleeve, where stripes appeared and disappeared as if by magic. "Private Malone."

"Stay clear of him," Wojensky warned Lumpy. "He likes his drinking and his fighting. I'm not sure which he favors more, but at least he fights good."

"Glad to meet you," Lumpy grinned.

"Stretch Dobbs," the tall man nodded.

"Holzer you've met."

Wolfgang clicked his heels and bowed. "Holzer you've met," he repeated.

"Want us to give you a hand with them spuds?" Stretch asked.

"We can handle 'em," Dutch grumbled. He hefted a sack, shouldered it, and then, puffing, hoisted another sack. He lumbered off, staggering under the weight of two hundred pounds of potatoes.

"Sure you don't want some help, Lumpy?"

"Naw." He glanced toward the kitchen. "I guess Sarge don't want you guys helpin' me."

As he spoke, Lumpy Torkleson had been picking up another sack of potatoes, so that he now had two on his right side, one over his shoulder, one under his arm. Turning around, he snatched up a sack with his left hand and stepped up onto the boardwalk and into the mess hall, whistling as he went.

"Goddamn," Stretch said reverently. "That big son of a bitch had three hundred pounds of spuds there. Like it was nothin'!"

"Did, didn't he," Malone chuckled.

Dutch Rothausen came back for a second load, mopping the perspiration from his brow despite the coolness of the evening.

Malone's eyes glinted devilishly. Leaning against the porch upright, arms crossed, he said to Dutch Rothausen, "Well, I just seen it."

"Seen what?"

"A man who can outmuscle Dutch Rothausen."

Before Dutch could respond, Wojensky added thoughtfully, "But then maybe that's not fair. After all, *Sergeant* Rothausen is getting just a tad past his prime now."

"Who the hell you talking about?" Dutch demanded, his pride stung by the remark. He puffed up like a bullfrog, as if to demonstrate that he had lost none of his raw strength. It was then that Torkleson came back out onto the porch, the lantern light shadowing his soft features.

"Him, you mean?" Dutch demanded. "Torkleson? He's only a pup, boys."

"If he is, he's a hell of a big one."

"Looks like he could show the old dog something," Wojensky said.

"Three bags, Dutch," Malone told him, nodding at Torkleson. "That man just walked in with three bags of spuds."

"The hell you say." Dutch squinted at Torkleson.

"I think he's got the edge, Dutch."

"Three bags ain't nothin'," Dutch decided. Then, to prove it, he loaded a bag on his shoulder, balanced it with the point of his chin, slipped a second bag under his arm, picked up a third, and staggered toward the doorway, his knees looking ready to buckle.

"Think you could carry four?" Malone asked Torkleson, walking slowly around him, studying the breadth of that huge back, the thick shoulders of Lumpy Torkleson.

"Ah," Lumpy waved a hand, "I don't want to get in no contest."

"It's not really a contest," Malone said, "it's just to show Rothausen something."

Torkleson was dubious. "I show him something, he's liable to show me something else. I'm liable to be scrubbing pots for the next six months."

"Wojensky won't let that happen, will you, Wo?"

"No. You're in my squad, Torkleson. Our squad. We'll look after you."

"I don't know," Torkleson said. "It ain't right to show off."

"You mean you *can* do it?"

"I reckon." He nodded his massive head slowly. "That's four hundred pounds, ain't it? I reckon so. Sure."

Malone and Stretch helped him out. Standing two bags on end, they held them as Torkleson stuffed two one-hundred-pound bags under either massive arm. Then, squatting slightly, he gripped the other two sacks with his meaty hands. He started to heft them, but Wojensky said, "Wait a minute. I'll give you the signal."

They waited until Rothausen reappeared in the doorway, his face red in the glare of the lantern. He was still puffing, but he managed a triumphant, "There!"

"Now," Wojensky said, and as Rothausen started to do a bit of bragging, Torkleson, with a grunt and a heave, lifted those four hundred—pound sacks of spuds and walked past Rothausen, whose jaw fell as Wojensky and the others burst into laughter.

"Looks like the sergeant ain't the post strongman any-more," Stretch said.

"It's age creeping up," Wojensky said. Rothausen stood there, angry, numb, and awed by turns.

"You know what it is, Sarge?" Malone asked.

"Not the Malone Theory again," Wojensky said.

"What's that?" Rothausen wanted to know.

"It's causing you to lose your strength now. That's the next sign."

"What in hell are you talking about, Malone!"

"Lack of sex," Malone said in a low voice. He bowed his head slightly, glancing around. "It makes a man lose it."

"You are full of shit, Malone."

"Sarge, it's true. So help me. Happened to my uncle. Biggest baddest brawlingest man in Ulster. Had him a little piece of fluff until she upped and run off with a brewery owner from Kildare. Plumb ruined him," Malone said with a sad shake of his head. "Hell, six months without a woman and he couldn't pluck a goose. Not long after, that poor, trembling wreck of a man just cashed in his chips."

Rothausen was ready to laugh, to fight, but somewhere deep inside he half believed Malone. "Really? Are you shitting me, Malone?"

"Sarge!" Malone looked hurt. "Would I joke about a thing like that?"

Lumpy Torkleson emerged from the mess hall, whistling, breathing easily. Rothausen frowned.

"Hell, I could do four hundred, but I got a bum hand," Dutch said. "You know that, Wojensky. From that Arapaho. Stabbed me clean through that meat hook." He held up the hand as evidence.

"Sure," Wojensky said; he didn't sound convinced.

"Dammit, it's true!" Dutch roared.

"I know it," Wojensky said even less believingly.

"By God, I'll show you!" Dutch fumed. Walking to the tailgate of the wagon, he turned, squatted, and eased back under the wagon. He found his grip and lifted, his shoulders braced beneath the planks of the bed.

His face went beet red, the veins on his neck bulged. It was obvious he was giving it his all, but the wagon never moved.

And Dutch never saw Malone, Stretch, and Holzer reach out and hold the wagon down as he tried valiantly to budge it. Wojensky stood directly in front of Dutch, distracting him and shaking his head as if it were a pitiful sight to see this once virile ox of a man in such a condition.

Finally, Dutch gave it up. Stepping out in a crouch, he straightened with a groan and shook his head as he eyed the wagon. His face dripped with sweat.

"Damn . . ." he panted. "I would've sworn . . ." He eyed Torkleson. "By God, let's see you do it!"

"Sarge, I don't want to—"

"That's an order!"

"Sarge."

"Do it!"

Torkleson nodded obediently and backed under the wagon. He shifted his weight, planted his feet, took a deep breath, let half of it out, and shoved. The rear end of the wagon came up smoothly and evenly.

Torkleson glanced sheepishly at Rothausen, lowered the wagon carefully, and stepped out, dusting his shoulders off.

"Well, goddammit!" Rothausen sputtered. Then he turned and stomped into the mess hall, slamming the door behind him.

They walked swiftly away, holding their laughter until

they were nearly back to the barracks. Only Torkleson seemed unamused.

"What's the matter, Lumpy? We got you out of there, didn't we?"

"That's a poor thing to do to somebody," Torkleson said with genuine sympathy.

"You might have gone too far," Stretch said.

"Hell, he deserved every bit of it, the way that man's been poisoning us," Wojensky decided. "That was brilliant, Malone. That theory of yours."

Malone was straight-faced. "I'm serious about that," he said.

"Come on! About your uncle and all?"

"Oh, that? No, I was just piling it on." Then he added seriously, "But I do think Dutch's mind is on his gonads and not on his cooking. I've seen it plenty of times. That man has the heavy-balls misery. We ain't going to get any decent eats until we've straightened him out."

"What's up?" Reb McBride asked as he came up to them, a despondent Cutter Grimes behind him.

They told him about it, and Reb listened with an ever-widening grin. "That was beautiful," he finally said. "And I'm with Malone. He deserved that."

"Thinking about Rothausen's problem," Malone said, "kind of gets a man to thinking about his own." His eyes drifted toward the lights in the sky. The calliope music played a siren song that drifted through the cool air.

"Think there's a chance?" Stretch asked wistfully.

"They got women," Malone said, slapping his back. "And where there's women there's hope. Let's get ourselves on over to this circus."

Lumpy Torkleson tried to beg off. He had spent three days in a coach and all day scrubbing pots, but they wouldn't hear of that.

"I haven't got a pass," he insisted.

"We'll get you through, don't worry," Reb said. "You're with us now. Best damned squad in the United States Army."

Torkleson was reluctant, Cutter Grimes somber, Holzer

eager but confused. There was no holding back the others. They wanted to see a show, hear some music, walk the midway.

And there was always that hope.

seven _____

There was a chill edge on the evening breeze as Matt Kincaid tapped at the door to Warner Conway's quarters. It was a moment before anyone answered, and Matt turned his back to the door, watching the hazy glow from the circus against the night sky. Someone shouted from far away, a joyous hoot.

The door opened and Flora Conway stood there, backlit by the soft lantern light, lovely, almost regal in a pale blue dress with little ruffled cuffs. She smiled warmly. "Dear Matt, come in, please."

She took his hand and led him into the parlor. There was a lingering, tantalizing scent that Matt recognized as Maggie Cohen's justly famous Irish stew. Conway was tilted back in his favorite chair, his legs crossed at the knee. And beside him sat Bates DeQueen, looking smug as usual, slightly bored.

"Evening, Matt," Conway said, rising. There was a note of relief in his voice. Matt shook the senior officer's hand.

"Mister DeQueen was telling us about his visit to the Indian agency," Flora said.

"It was enlightening," DeQueen allowed, "but as I have just finished explaining to the captain, it's hardly enough for me to be guided around by the hand, introduced to some tame Indians, and told war stories."

Matt felt the heat rising in his face and neck. Turkey Creek Island was not just another "war story" to Matt Kincaid, and he resented having it described so.

"I can understand your enthusiasm, DeQueen," Conway said, "your professional curiosity. But I am afraid, as you have been told repeatedly, that our rules must be adhered to. You speak of 'tame Indians.' I am afraid that those are the only ones you could speak to with any expectation of survival."

"I can't accept that, sir," DeQueen insisted. "They would certainly see that I mean them no harm. An intelligent chief—like Elk Tooth, for instance—would see that I could be useful in explaining the position of the Cheyenne and Sioux nations in this conflict."

"It would never get that far, sir," Kincaid said abruptly.

"Men don't kill for sport."

"No?" Matt shook his head.

"You would be branded as the enemy by your skin color, Mr. DeQueen," Captain Conway explained. "The Cheyenne are taking no prisoners of war."

"I can't believe it."

"You will have to, sir," Captain Conway said firmly. "Knowing Matt as I do, I have to think that a part of the reason he mentioned Turkey Creek, which I know he is reluctant to discuss, is so that the idea that there are actually real, bloody hostiles out there might sink in. You seem to believe they are wild game running the plains, and we are the hunters."

"I have formed no firm opinions, sir," DeQueen shot back. "I hardly can, until I have reached an understanding of both sides' positions."

Flora Conway, who, like any good officer's wife, never interfered or spoke up when her husband talked war, now stepped in, seeing that both Warner and Matt Kincaid were slowly losing their composure again.

"Coffee, gentlemen?" she asked. She glanced at Warner as she stepped between the men, setting the little silver coffee service on the table. Conway nodded slightly.

"Matt?" she offered.

"No, thank you. I only came to report that Mr. Taylor has sent a rider in, sir. No contact with Elk Tooth."

"Mr. Taylor?" DeQueen asked.

"Second Lieutenant Taylor," Conway said. "He's out where I expect you wish you were, pursuing Elk Tooth. Very well, Matt."

"Anything else, sir?"

80

"No, nothing. Mr. DeQueen has talked me into drawing up Little Big Horn and explaining it to him later on. Unless you have a special interest in staying, maybe you could use a night off yourself. Join the boys over at the circus, maybe."

"I might," Matt answered. He glanced once more at DeQueen, "unless you would prefer me to stay."

"No." Warner rose, putting a hand on Matt's shoulder. "It's not necessary, Matt." They walked to the door and Warner Conway said in a low voice, "I only wish to hell I was going with you."

Then he slapped Matt's shoulder, smiled thinly, and returned to his chair as Matt stepped out into the cool evening, closing the door behind him. There was some kind of a squabble at the gate and Matt turned that way, finding Privates Perry and Watts arguing quietly but firmly with a civilian.

Matt recognized her, smiled, and went over. Private Watts glanced up and saluted, and nodded to the civilian.

"Good evening, sir. Trying to explain to this woman that she's not allowed on post."

It was Quail Song, standing there squat and forlorn, her belongings in a sack at her side. Glancing back toward the captain's quarters , Matt experienced a momentary urge to let the Indian woman through.

"You can't come in, Quail Song," Matt told her. Then, in Cheyenne, he repeated the order. She shook her head miserably, turned up those big round eyes, and her lip trembled.

"What's this about, Lieutenant?" Perry asked.

"She's looking for a man," Matt told them. Both of them took a step back, looking away. "Get along now, Quail Song," Matt said, shooing her gently back. "Go home."

She picked up her sack and withdrew some twenty feet from the gate, where she sat perched on a smooth rock, staring sadly at them.

Matt shook his head. "You boys got some relief coming later?" he asked Perry and Watts.

"Too late," Perry said wistfully. "I guess we'll have to go tomorrow night. There's supposed to be a second show."

"Tough luck. Good evening, boys."

"Evenin', sir."

Perry and Watts saluted and Matt walked through the gate, angling toward the lights, the music, the laughter.

Of course there would be a second performance, maybe a third. Milo Grimaldi would know that half of the troops would not be able to get away. And unless they had come through town, which Matt didn't think was the case, it would take a while for all those folks to arrive. Time for the kids to wheedle and whine, for momma to beg, for dad to throw down his saw or hammer or shovel in disgust, get into that hard-collared Sunday shirt, and drive on over.

The first performance in the big tent was already concluded before Matt arrived. Stretch, Reb, Holzer, Torkleson, and Grimes, along with Malone and Wojensky, had spilled out onto the midway, laughing and remarking upon the girl who rode the horses standing up and upside down, the clown in the tiny trunk, the probability that the lion had teeth, the daredevil who dove into the small tub of water from the tower, and whether or not the knife-thrower had ever pinned his assistant to that slanted board.

There were a few townies, some agency Indians, and a whole lot of blue coats wandering the midway now, listening to the barkers, squinting into the glare of those lanterns that had mirrors behind them to increase their intensity, the kids munching candy apples, the sodbusters with rifles in hand, standing hipshot, glaring sourly at the circus people and soldiers alike.

"Come on over here," Malone said. He nodded toward the shadow behind the big tent.

"What for?"

"Come on," Malone repeated, crooking his little finger. They followed him a few steps back into the darkness, and when they were gathered around, he produced with great flair a quart bottle of whiskey.

"Where'd you get that?" Wojensky wanted to know.

"Don't look a gift horse in the mouth, Corp."

Reb took the bottle and downed a healthy swallow, setting his throat to burning, his eyes to watering. "Damn, Malone," he gasped. "You'd better stay clear of that. A man who can get loose on three-point-two beer has no business playing with that."

Malone grinned, took a drink, wiped the bottle with his shirtsleeve, and offered it to Wojensky, who took a drink and passed it on, shuddering as it hit bottom.

"Where did you get that?"

"Pop Evans," Malone shrugged.

"The hell you say. He's not supposed to do that. Only that three-point-two beer."

"You know Pop," Malone said.

"His ass would be on the line if the captain found out," Reb said. He pondered that, looking at Cutter Grimes, who was taking a long swig, his Adam's apple bobbing. "Maybe we could use that to get Cutter off the hook."

"The hell!" Malone said emphatically. "Then where would we get whiskey?"

"No, Reb," Cutter agreed. "I told you, it's my problem, and none of your'n. I don't mean to be the cause of the whiskey gettin' cut off."

"All right." It was Reb's turn again, and he took a quick, furtive drink, feeling the glow begin to move through muscles and ligaments, bone and blood. "But it's still *our* problem, son. All of ours, and we'll find a way."

"Ain't but two days left," Cutter said. He took another deep, deep drink and Malone said nothing. Cutter likely needed it tonight. Damn shame, Malone thought, with a woman waiting at home and all. He glanced at Reb and then at Wojensky, who shook his head.

"Come on, then," Malone boomed, throwing an arm around Lumpy and Reb's shoulders. "Let's have us a time!"

They wandered the midway then, passing the sideshows and concession stands. Reb bought a candy apple and munched on it; the lights spun around him slightly as the whiskey began to work. Malone was already stewed, and Reb let him wander on ahead, holding Cutter back as well.

"There'll be a fight within an hour, and Malone will be front and center when it starts. I don't have the mood on me for that."

They could see Stretch shouldering toward a game where

folks tossed rings over blocks of wood for prizes. That looked simple enough, but Reb hadn't noticed anybody winning much, outside of a few cheap plaster banks.

"Let's have a look at this, Cutter," Reb suggested.

The tent before them was gaudily painted and advertised to all that inside were the world's most beautiful Siamese twins. Their portraits stared out across the prairie, two young blond women riding a specially made side-by-side twin bicycle. There was a deal of well-turned leg showing.

They wanted a nickel admission, and Cutter held back. "You go ahead, Reb. I'll see how Stretch is doing."

"You sure?"

"Sure."

Reb slapped him on the back, called him a good ol' boy, and slapped his nickel on the barker's table. The man's voice echoed across the midway.

". . . Nature's tragic error, a shocking miscarriage of biological intent, the two young and luscious women pathetically and irremediably joined at the hip . . ."

Reb shouldered on into the tent, eased along the bench, which was already crowded with curiosity-seekers, and took his seat just as the lanterns were lowered and the curtain raised.

They had a little warmup act consisting of two midget jugglers and a little white dog that could do two backward somersaults. It was warm and close in the tent, and Reb jammed a fist up before his gaping yawn as the whiskey lulled him to a doze.

Then the jugglers were gone and a drum roll brought up a second, faded blue curtain, and Reb's eyes came open wide, his sleepiness passing instantly.

They came forward to the riffle of applause. Reb had figured they would be just a little overripe, just a little old. But by God they were beautiful, long-legged, juicy, and sweet to behold.

"Ava and Anna Boles," the barker shouted.

Two blonds, both amazingly pretty, yet their hips were locked together. It didn't dampen their spirits any, however. Wearing twin yellow bathing outfits that dropped only to their knees, they kicked up their heels and, smiling all the while, swung into a nice rendition of "Mother was a Sailor."

Reb was mesmerized, overwhelmed, turned upside down and twisted. He let his eyes roam over them—or was it *she*?—from their bobbing blond tresses to their little yellow slippers.

Which one decided what they would do, which way to go, when to sleep? One brain or two? They danced on, and Reb's thoughts turned to less scientific interests.

Did they have one? Or two? There were four legs, so it must be two. Four tits! The whiskey had him perplexed, heated up, and wildly curious. Reb worked his way along the side of the tent, despite an occasional "Sit down!" from the folks in the crowd, and he stood, bleary-eyed, in front of the stage, wondering how it would be. Did they ever? Two men or one?

They turned and started dancing a jig, and Reb's eyes swept up those long, smooth calves to their hips. Those hips, swinging in musical tandem, sensuous synchronism. If a man . . . he blinked, wiped his eyes, and swallowed hard as the twins turned and the one on the left winked.

Most definitely, warmly winked.

He had never been winked at by a Siamese twin before, but damned if it didn't look like a single woman's wink, the kind that meant "take a closer look." He rested his elbows on the stage and dreamed on.

A faint scent of lavender drifted to his nostrils and Reb felt a stirring in his crotch. Even joined at the hip, even with a sisterly chaperone always there, didn't they have a normal, healthy woman's appetite? They turned, spun in a tight circle, and bowed away. The curtain dropped, but not before that head on the left had winked again, most definitely, and blown Reb a kiss.

The curtain dropped and he heard the squeak and shuffle of feet behind him. Yet he was in no hurry to leave. There were times when a man had to take little voyages of discovery if he wanted to find a new world.

Reb turned and slowly walked out, his head turned back across his shoulder, the barker urging him along as the lanterns were turned up again.

Outside it was cold, clear. Cutter Grimes was gone, as

were the rest of the boys. Reb turned one way, halted at the corner of the tent, and pondered. Then, when the barker was looking the other way, he slipped back inside and scurried down the empty aisle, climbing onto the stage. There was no one watching, and after a quick glance behind him, Reb went behind the curtain. The scent of lavender grew stronger.

Matt Kincaid had missed the big show, and he didn't feel much like games of chance, although he saw a farmer with a box of cigars he had won by ringing the bell at the Tower of Strength. Slamming the mallet down on a wooden, hinged paddle drove a brass cylinder up along a cable past variously colored segments with various legends, such as "Lightweight," "Sissy," "A Real Man," "Hercules," and so on until the bell was reached.

That farmer had a dollar box of cigars, but he must have spent two winning them, which was obviously the whole idea of the game. Kincaid had an idea it was fixed, although he couldn't tell just how.

He saw a knot of his soldiers walking toward him, and to save them having to salute, Matt turned to one side and found himself before a poster that announced The Dance of the Seven Veils.

"The mysterious and delectable Delilah," the ticket seller said. "Performing the exotic and ancient dance of the pharaoh's concubine. You don't want to miss this, Lieutenant."

Matt shrugged. He could take it or leave it. Yet he needed something to get him into the spirit of things. There was little point in coming over, wandering around, and seeing nothing, so he handed the ticket seller a nickel, receiving a yellow ticket and a leering smile in return.

He had planned on sitting in the back, but for some reason the only seat left was dead front and center. Matt eased down there and sat, his head tilted back slightly.

Backstage, Arturo Mercator was having his fourth fit of jealousy that afternoon. Carla Bramante, draped in sheer veils and little else, adjusted the little golden crown she wore on her head.

"You said you wouldn't do this again," Arturo said. He

hopped around her like an agitated frog, behind the mirror, beside her, his hands pleading, on his knees, his eyes prayerful.

"Gerta is sick," Carla explained for the tenth time. "Someone has to do it."

"Let the people go home. Let them have their money back."

"I'm sure Milo would like that," Carla said, her dark eyes flashing. "You're silly again, Arturo. You promised not to be silly again."

"Look at you," he exclaimed righteously. "All the men seeing your body, your legs, my God! My future wife."

"That is not settled," she snapped. Standing, she raised the veil across her eyes.

"I beg you, Carla." Arturo became more dramatic. "I'll kill myself!"

"Don't be so silly," she said, casually pushing by him as she received her cue from out front.

"I forbid it!" Arturo grabbed her arm roughly, and her searing gaze met his. She shook away angrily.

"You can forbid me nothing. You can order me to do nothing!

"I am my own woman, not your wife. I do what I want, I go where I want."

"Dance shamelessly when you want!" he shouted.

"Yes."

"Make a whore of yourself!"

He had gone too far. That dark, level gaze settled on him and she said coldly, "Whatever I wish, Arturo. You think I act like a whore? Maybe I will show you how a whore acts, eh? Eh, Arturo?" She put her hands on his chest and pushed. He backed away and she followed, repeating the motion. "What you think? Carla should show you?"

Arturo swallowed an answer, shook his head, and tried to speak, but his throat was dry and Carla's cue was repeated.

The lanterns were dimmed and Carla turned toward the stage, her veils swirling around her long legs as she moved with an emphatic swaying of her hips to her position.

To the relentless beat of an accompanying drum played

by a young male member of the troupe, dressed in what looked like an oversized diaper, his body smeared with burnt cork, the obvious intention of which was to make him look like a "Nubian," but which only succeeded in making him look as though he'd spent the night sleeping in a coal bin.

Carla flitted onto the stage, moving with the grace of a doe, the sensuous fluidity of "the pharaoh's concubine." Her eyes sparked, her long neck arched back as her legs flashed. Arturo watched from behind the curtain, grinding his teeth in jealous frustration.

Carla was aware of Arturo's watching eyes, aware of all the male eyes on her, and she flounced, swayed, swung her hips, and bent low, her breasts swinging lazily as she parted her lips and let her head loll from side to side in blatant sexuality.

Arturo was enraged and Carla knew it. Just then she didn't care. The dance was an act of liberation, and she wound her fingers in her dark hair, closing her eyes as she swayed.

Her eyes fell on the tall, dark officer in the front row. Handsome he was, rugged and confident looking. Carla let her eyes settle on him and she performed for him and him alone as if it were a dance of seduction, and her body warmed to the thought, it became exactly that, on an unconscious level at first, and then on a very conscious, intense level.

She swayed, went to her knees, arched her back, and let her hands flow in vague, sinuous gestures as her breasts rose and fell with the exertion of the sexual charade.

Carla rose, kicked out, stripped off a veil and then another as the drumbeat increased, and she found herself not so much dancing as presenting her body to Matt Kincaid, exhibiting its lush curves, its functional aspects.

She went to her belly and writhed forward to draw nearer to Matt Kincaid. Carla licked her lips slowly, her hips rising and falling in unmistakable sexual simulation.

Matt felt his blood begin to move a little quicker. If this was the regular show, it was a wonder some sheriff somewhere hadn't locked them up.

Carla rolled to her side, her hips still rolling, her mouth

partly open, her eyes glassy and fixed on Matt Kincaid as she whispered words that did not reach the audience.

Abruptly the drum stopped, and she leaped to her bare feet and ran from the stage, leaving the audience stunned. Then there was a rolling wave of applause and Matt, with the others, got to his feet and walked slowly out of the tent.

There was some kind of ruckus off across the circus grounds, and Matt thought he heard Malone's bellowing voice, and he started that way. Then he heard another fight, nearer, harsher.

A woman screamed, and Matt turned toward the back of the tent.

She was there beneath the oaks, still dressed in those veils, and an angry young man had her by the wrist. He yelled something in a foreign language and she slapped at him, twisting and turning, her fingernails clawing at his eyes.

Matt stepped out of the shadows.

"Anything wrong?" he asked.

"Nothing that concerns you," Arturo Mercator snapped. "Get your blue butt out of here."

"He's hurting me," Carla complained. She tried to unbend his fingers from around her wrist, but Arturo was hanging on tight. "Let me go!" She turned to Matt. "Help me!"

Matt knew it was always a bad situation to horn in between a man and his woman when they were fighting. Yet the girl's eyes were pleading, and the man really seemed to be hurting her now as his fingers dug into that shapely wrist.

"Best let her go," Matt said mildly.

"Go to hell!"

"I'm asking you nice," Matt said. "Whatever it is, you can talk it out."

"I don't talk to this pig. He is no one to me!" Carla shrieked.

"He's not your husband?"

"He's no one, a pig. Stop it, Arturo, you're hurting me!"

"Friend," Matt Kincaid warned him, "let go. I'm not telling you again."

Then Arturo did let go, flinging Carla to the ground. Matt saw the flash of silver moonlight on a knife blade, and he managed to step aside as Arturo lunged at him.

Matt grabbed the man's shirtsleeve as the knife lashed out, and stuck out his boot and yanked Arturo forward. The fellow's own impetus drove him into the oak tree beyond Matt. Arturo hit the tree with his skull, started to rise, then collapsed to the earth with a little sigh.

Matt walked to him, picked up the knife, and heaved it into the brush at the perimeter of the clearing. Then he walked to Carla, who sat against the dark, cold earth, her eyes moon-bright.

"You all right?" Matt asked.

"I don't know." Her eyes were still filled with residual liquid fire, the fire of The Dance of the Seven Veils. She glanced once at Arturo, who lay peacefully against the ground.

"Maybe you can help me back to my wagon," she suggested. "I feel shaky. I'm not sure I can stand."

Matt almost believed her. He bent down, scooped her up and carried her in the direction she indicated. She leaned her head against his shoulder, and Matt felt the gentle touch of her soft hair against his throat, felt the smooth flesh through the flimsy costume, the slightly quickened breathing of Carla Bramante near his ear.

There was no way in the world he was going to notice the two Cheyenne creeping up the riverbed toward the circus.

eight _____

The tent was set back from the circus grounds proper.
A light showed dimly through the heavy canvas. The sounds
of feminine murmuring floated through the air. Reb halted
uncertainly. It was cool and damp. The breeze along the
riverbed thrust cold hands inside his uniform, frisking him.
This was a crazy idea, a wild notion, he told himself. But
the lower half of his body urged him forward.

He would just have to wing it, finding some sort of spur-
of-the-moment excuse. He walked the last three strides to
the tent. As he stood there, his teeth began to chatter from
the cold. He lifted a hand and rapped on the wooden tent
frame.

The murmuring stopped. He heard a creak, a scraping
sound, and then the door opened a crack.

"Yes?"

Her hair was down, brushed to a gloss, shining in the
lantern light, and Reb swallowed hard. Just beside her face
was another equally beautiful face, and he muttered, "I just
wanted to . . . tell you I enjoyed your singin'. I wondered
if I couldn't get your autographs." His eyes went from one
smiling face to the other. Which one did you talk to?

The woman on the right, the one that had winked at Reb,
said, "Sure. Come on in." He did so, hat in hand, hesitantly
ducking through into the large, well-furnished tent.

They were as beautiful as ever in the dim lantern light,
wearing a blue dressing gown made for four arms. Reb
wondered momentarily if this all wasn't some mad delusion
caused by Pop Evans' bad whiskey.

"Thank you, ma'am," Reb mumbled. He rolled his hat
up in his hands and offered a shy smile.

91

"Just call me Ava," the right head said. "This is Anna."

"Reb," he drawled.

"Reb." One hand came out to meet his, and they shook hands. The hand was soft, and when she withdrew it, it was a slow parting, the touch of fingertips gentle against his rough palm.

"Would you like a drink, Reb?"

"Well, yes'm, if it ain't a lot of bother."

"None at all. We have some brandy, if you drink it."

"Only when I get the chance, ma'am, which ain't often."

"Please, call me Ava," that right head insisted. The left head—Anna—hadn't said anything. It just sort of sat there smiling. "Excuse us for a moment," Ava said.

Reb nodded and watched at they turned and walked behind a blanket that divided the tent into two nearly equal sections.

"Well?" Ava whispered.

"You like him."

"He's cute," she said, peeking back through the blanket. Reb stood uncertainly in the center of the room.

"Then why do you want to do it to him?" Anna asked.

"It's more fun," Ava said, and Anna nodded. "Besides," she went on, "it'll keep him a little off balance, and that's the way I like men."

"You're devilish," Anna whispered, holding back a laugh. "How are we going to handle it?"

"Just follow my lead. You don't have to do a thing," Ava told her sister.

"You'll outgrow this one day," Anna admonished her with a little giggle and a poke in the ribs.

"Sh! He'll hear."

"All right." Anna straightened up, assumed that vacant smile, and watched as Ava picked up the brandy bottle and three glasses.

Reb was starting to get itchy. His head came around sharply as the Siamese twins reentered the room, Ava carrying the brandy.

"Sit down," she encouraged him.

There was a worn blue velvet settee in one corner, and Reb eased down into it. Ava turned down the lantern a little, explaining cheerfully, "Coal oil's not cheap."

"No."

He watched with faint trepidation and more than a little excitement as they turned in unison and backed to the settee, sitting so that Ava was beside Reb, her firm, ripe hip brushing his as she sat. The robe they wore was loose, and as they settled, Reb's eyes caught a glimpse of a milk-white, smooth, and enticing breast. Whose, he was not certain. He felt confused and oddly warm, and the brandy Ava poured him did nothing to ease the confusion, but it settled him pleasantly and he found himself grinning for no apparent reason.

He noticed that Anna had said nothing, that although Ava had poured a drink for her, she had not picked it up. "Don't she drink?" Reb inquired, leaning forward to look across Ava at her sister.

"When I feel like it," Ava said. "You see, darling Reb, Anna is just another part of my body. Like you having another arm."

"But I seen her dance, smile, sing."

"Yes, but she's completely under my control. At times," she sighed, leaning back, "I think of having her sawn off and thrown away. But one doesn't cut off one's own arm, does one?"

Anna jabbed her sister sharply in the ribs, but her wooden smile didn't change. Ava let her hand slide down and rest on Reb's leg, and the gentle pressure of her fingers set his blood to racing. His cock came to a hopeful half-mast. He tossed down his brandy in a gulp.

"You mean she's not really there . . . here with us?" Reb wanted to know.

"We're alone, darling Reb. Just the two of us. Anna has no sensations beyond those of an animal, hardly any intelligence."

Anna's elbow jabbed Ava again, harder, and Ava struggled to keep a straight face. Her lips were slightly parted, her eyes hooded, sensuous. Reb shifted uncertainly in his seat, the brandy warming him, the hand on his thigh heating his brain.

"You mean she's just a part of you?" Reb asked, trying to clarify it.

"Oh yes. I have complete control. If I want her to dance,

93

she dances. Does she make you uncomfortable, dear Reb?" Her hand went to his cheek, cool, soft. Reb felt that heat climbing up into his neck. The tips of his ears burned.

"Well, it is kind of funny," he admitted, looking at Anna again uncertainly.

"I'll close her eyes," Ava said, and Anna, taking the cue, closed her eyes. "Pay no attention to her, Reb."

Ava's mouth lifted to his. Sweet, supple, faintly tasting of brandy, her lips met his, teasing his lower lip, opening to meet his lips in a fuller kiss.

Reb swallowed hard. She leaned back and looked at him with an intense, yet faraway gaze. Her hand tightened on his thigh and slowly crept up, not quite making it to his cock, which throbbed with an instant need.

He kissed her again, his lips going to her smooth throat. He nuzzled her breasts, his mouth finding the soft, warm cleavage where her robe opened. He could feel her pulse beneath his lips. Her head was tilted back, inviting his kisses.

Anna, her eyes closed, lifted her drink and sipped at it. Reb paused, glanced at Ava, and said, "Are you sure she . . . ?"

"I just thought another drink would be nice," Ava said, nipping at his earlobe as she put her arm around his shoulders. "This mouth was busy."

She purred, opened her mouth to his, slid her pink tongue between his lips, and then withdrew, saying, "That coal oil is very expensive, Reb. Maybe you should just turn that lantern off."

He rose, aware of her eyes on his crotch, where his growing erection strained at the fabric of his trousers. With a trembling hand he turned the wick down and the lantern went dark.

Feeling his way in the darkness, he found Ava standing, her robe open, and his mouth went to those nearly round, firm breasts, his tongue searching the taut nipples. Then she took his hand.

"In there," she said, breathing into his ear. Her breath was rapid, warm, moist. Reb's legs wobbled a little as he

94

followed her through the curtain into the inner compartment that was their—her—kitchen. There was a small wood-stove, a portable cupboard, and in the corner a wide bed with a blue silk bedspread and four overstuffed pillows.

That brandy, on top of the whiskey Malone had given him, had stoked a glowing fire in Reb's brain. The room swirled. Ava's voice reached him through a soft, fuzzy tunnel. Beckoning, she called his name softly, and Reb shed his shirt, nearly tripping as he pulled at his boots.

It was cold, standing naked in that breezy tent, but Ava had the blankets pulled back and he slid in beside her, snuggling against her warmth. Her hands roamed Reb's body. Her fingers ran down his spine, his buttocks, his thighs, and he rolled over for her.

Her fingers ran up his inner thigh and hesitated, and Reb could hardly endure the waiting until she stopped her teasing and her warm hand encircled his pulsing erection.

He moved closer to her, their mouths locked together as her hand slid gently over the length of his cock, pausing at the head of it to make a skilled, inflaming caress with the palm of her hand.

As her palm ran across it, Reb's cock twitched, filled with demanding needles of sensation. Then her hand dropped down the shaft, her thumb and forefinger smoothly stroking him until, reaching the base of his erection, she cupped his scrotum in her hand. Her breath was warm and rapid, and Reb placed his hand on her soft inner thigh, letting it find its way up to the warm, dewy cleft above.

His hands searched Ava's body, the silken skin, the crevices and contours. Her muscle tone was amazing beneath that film of soft skin, that thin layer of feminine fat.

This is it, Anna thought. Now how was Ava going to keep him from discovering the wood and harness leather apparatus which kept them joined during the act?

But she had underestimated her sister. Ava took Reb's right hand and intertwined it with her own left, and with her right she held his left to her eager, moist cleft.

Reb's brain was humming, but it was no longer the liquor that caused it. It was the scent of the woman, her lips against his lips. He moved forward, positioning his cock, and together their hands groped and stroked the head of it against Ava's clitoris, letting it dip half an inch inside of her until Reb could no longer wait and he tensed, driving it into her juicy depths.

She gasped and her hips began to sway, to writhe, and she drove her pelvis against his, murmuring soft words into his ear. Their hands still met at her crotch, their fingers stroking his shaft as it dipped and slithered, reaching a pulsing crest.

Her lips were on his face. Lips, ears, eyes, throat. Her hand gripped his hand tightly, their other hands touching, probing. The other hand slid across his ass and cupped his balls.

The other hand?

She was using three hands and then four, as another hand joined the two at her crotch, probing, stroking. It was a dream, a mad dream, with her hands touching his ass, his cock, his balls. He stroked her deeply, not thinking about it, but only feeling it. He kissed Ava's moist, trembling lips. The scent of her body filled his nostrils and sharpened his desire still more.

He kissed Ava's breasts, felt a mouth kissing his neck, another his chest. A hand took his head and guided it to Anna's breasts. Her nipples were taut and dark and he suckled greedily.

But Ava wanted him back, and she drew his head to her as Anna's hands slipped between his legs, her fingers clutching at him as he slid out of Ava, bringing her juices with him.

Ava's hands went to his buttocks and she clenched him to her, her teeth grinding as the throaty sounds she had been murmuring rose to a shriek of delight, a grunt, her hips writhing and slamming against him until Reb could no longer hold back and he fell into her thrusting, rolling rhythm, then halted, holding himself perfectly still as she continued to work.

He held himself away from her a few inches, and the hands stroked and manipulated him as Ava's inner muscles milked him and he sagged forward with a shudder, coming with a rush.

He lay there slick with perspiration, her scent and his mingled in the air as her juices mingled with his, as the tender hands ran up his spine, along his buttocks, over his shoulders, as he and Ava locked in a deep, finishing kiss.

His breathing settled and his heart slowed. He stroked her long blond hair, kissed her forehead, her chin. She ran her hands down his back and her thighs moved against his, and Reb felt his cock begin to stir, to grow again. It had been a long time, a damned long time.

He smiled in the darkness, swayed against her, and began a lazy, gentle thrusting.

"You're good to me, Reb," Ava said, touching her finger to his lips. "I liked it. Oh, that's good. A little higher." She gurgled pleasurably. "You're a big man and tender." Her hand found his balls and cupped them tenderly, and she said, "I think I'd like it in the other one this time."

He stopped, frozen. "In the other one?"

"My other pussy, dear man."

"I thought—" he paused. What had he thought? What was this, a nightmare or a dream to end all dreams?

"This one's a little tired, Reb." She kissed his ear, then she kissed both ears. One mouth stayed with an ear, whispering, "Love me again, just as good. Just as good," and the other mouth found his shoulder, gently nibbling at it.

He withdrew his cock, missing the warmth of her body instantly. Yet hands guided him and Anna's thighs spread, her knees lifting as he settled against her, sliding slowly inside as her mouth came up hungrily, energetically. "I can't wait," Ava said from over there.

Reb plunged in, finding her wet and ready, and she rolled against him, pressing herself against his pelvis. Slowly Anna's—Ava's?—legs lifted as she began to breath audibly, hoarsely through her mouth. Reb felt his need rising again and she urged him on, her legs thrust into the air, her nails digging into his ass as other hands encouraged his cock, played with Ava's rigid clitoris, as their bodies squeaked and swayed and slid against each other and the blood rose in Reb's temples until he though his head was going to burst and he reached a hard, debilitating, loin-devastating climax the instant Anna found hers.

She grappled and tore at him, her teeth clamping down

hard on his shoulder as she came undone inside, the muscles flexing, swelling, throbbing, going slack as their bodies slurped and pounded together.

Reb lay against her, gasping as she continued to sway, to roll, to claw, to kiss. Finally she settled, her voice going to a little humming, tuneless song as her light fingers traced patterns on his back.

"When you get your breath, darling," Ava said. She leaned over and kissed his cheek as Anna kissed his chest, her teeth plucking hairs from it.

"When what?" he panted. He was drained, beat-up, bruised, and dry. Her hand slid to his ass, gently caressing it, tracing the line of the crease there. She leaned far forward and kissed his ass.

"When you have a minute to regain your breath," Ava repeated. She kissed his ear, her tongue tracing the whorl of it. She smiled. "Then I'd like it again. In *this* one."

"I can't," Reb breathed. Her hand rested reassuringly on his ass.

"Sure you can, Reb, just rest a minute. Just a minute, sugar." And as the four hands got back to work, the four lips kissed him, the four smooth thighs swayed against him, as Anna hummed with peaceful satisfaction and Ava coaxed him, he began to think that maybe he could.

"It was nice of you to step in back there," Carla said. She handed Matt Kincaid a cup of coffee and perched on the edge of a table, sipping her own cup, her long, dancer's legs dangling.

"It wasn't much." Matt shrugged. "What was it, Carla? A lovers' spat?"

She glanced down, staring into her coffee. "Yes, I guess so. He's always assumed we would be married one day, and so Arturo treats me like a wife. Tonight he made me angry and so I made him angry. A little too angry, it seems."

"You're a beautiful woman, Carla. I can't blame a man for being jealous over you."

"Thank you." She smiled at Matt. Her face was soft now, the animal sensuality faded. Her mouth was full, straight white teeth behind sensitive lips. Her eyes were dark, pen-

98

etrating. "I have two more performances tonight, one in fifteen minutes, Matt. If I didn't—"

"That wouldn't be any good, Carla. Not just to make Arturo jealous. It could get somebody hurt."

"It wouldn't be to make Arturo jealous, Matt. You're a hell of a good-looking man, you know." Her eyes met his proudly, challengingly, and he only nodded.

"Thanks for the compliment."

"Tomorrow night I will be off early. Maybe I will see you tomorrow night, Matt Kincaid."

He rose, put on his hat, and placed his coffee cup on the table. "By tomorrow, you and Arturo will be two lovebirds again."

"Maybe. Maybe so, and maybe not, Matt." She rose to her tiptoes and kissed his cheek, then whispered, "Why don't you come back and find out?"

"That might not be the best idea."

"I am afraid he might hurt me. Come back, Matt," she said, pouting quite insincerely.

He watched her for a long moment, took in that raven-black, glossy hair, the proud tilt of her head, the deep eyes and long, perfect legs.

"All right," he agreed. "Just to check on you."

"Just to check," she answered. "You won't forget?" she asked, opening the door.

"Not likely." Then he kissed her. He put his arm around her, felt her go loose and then respond strongly, and he knew he would definitely be back.

Arturo was lurking in the shadows and he pressed back against a tree as Matt stepped down, touched his hatbrim, and strode away.

"I kill you, you son of a bitch," Arturo muttered to the night. His eyes were hot, drilling into Matt Kincaid's back as the officer strode away. "I swear, blue-butt, Arturo Mercator will kill you for this."

nine _____

Cutter Grimes and Wojensky stood watching a dirt farmer, a bull of a man, bang away at the Tower of Strength. He would muscle up, spit on his hands, plant his feet, and swing with that practiced stroke of a hard-rock miner or a man used to a pick.

He was a big-shouldered man with grim determination on his face. His blood vessels bulged, his eyes narrowed with concentration as the tiny red-haired woman with him watched with fading pride, expectant hopefulness.

"Hit 'er again, Moose!" the operator of the Tower would encourage him. A brittle sort of encouragement it was, half challenge, half mockery. The little man wore a striped red and yellow coat, smoked a thin cigar, and leaned on a bamboo cane. "The little lady wants to see you ring that bell. How about it, little lady, you want to see the big man win a kewpie doll for you, don't you?"

She murmured something under her breath. A birdlike squeak. The farmer glowered at the operator and looked up to the bell at the very pinnacle of the Tower of Strength.

"One more time," he said angrily. He handed the circus man another nickel, hefted the hammer, and with an explosive grunt brought the huge wooden mallet down, putting all of his considerable weight behind it.

The brass cylinder took off like a shot, riding the steel cable upward as the farmer's eyes followed it. Abruptly it stopped and descended, after labeling the farmer "Plowboy." The crowd roared with laughter, the farmer fumed, the little lady turned her eyes downward.

"I don't care for a kewpie doll, Horace," she murmured in her bird voice.

"No, dammit! I'll do it." He unpeeled his coat and tossed it aside, spitting on his hands again.

"It's all a matter of leverage, sir," the operator said. "Rock up on the balls of your feet. Nice easy swing."

The farmer looked dubiously at the narrow man, shook his head, and tried to comply with the instructions. The brass cylinder exploded off the wooden paddle and impacted with the bell, and a satisfying ring echoed across the midway.

"There you are," the operator said, beaming. "I knew a man built like you could handle that." With a flourish, he handed the kewpie doll to the little lady. She thanked him uncertainly, took Horace's arm, and was escorted away. Horace swaggered a bit with masculine pride now, though he muttered, "Damn doll cost me a dollar and a half."

"Who's next?" the Tower of Strength operator wanted to know. "Show the little lady what kind of man you are."

"That's got to be a rig," Cutter Grimes said.

"Sure it is," Wojensky agreed. "And I'll tell you how it's done. Once, back in Ohio, I worked for a carnival. That cable there, the one the cylinder rides on. If it's taut, that clapper will ride right up it. Give it a little slack and that elephant we saw couldn't drive it up. Look," Wojensky said with a barely perceptible nod. "There's a pedal near the barker's foot. When he looks to be leaning casual up against that tower, he either steps on it or not, taking up the slack. The trick is to know when to let a man win. I've seen some mighty big men get mighty mad. Usually their pride will keep them trying, especially if they're with a woman. Then, after they've more than paid for some trinket or other, the operator lets them win and walk away feeling like a king."

"It seems like a risky little con," Cutter said. "Take a man like Dutch Rothausen. Damn, would he ever blow his stack!"

"Wouldn't he?" Wojensky scratched his chin, a slow, malicious grin creeping onto his face. "Just a minute, Cutter. I want to talk to this man."

Cutter frowned and watched as Wojensky swaggered over, took the Tower of Strength operator aside, and whispered to him. He seemed to be explaining something. The operator nodded, looking around. Then Cutter saw the two men shake hands in that special way men had when something was changing hands.

"All right, my boy," Wojensky said. "Let's see the rest of that midway."

Wojensky was whistling as they walked, and Cutter asked him, "All right, Wo. What's up?"

"Nothing, my boy. Nothing at all."

Cutter hardly heard the response. He had stopped short suddenly beside the bearded lady's tent. Wojensky had to retrace his steps.

"What is it, Cutter?"

Cutter Grimes was staring across the midway, his mouth set in a tight, humorless smile, his eyes narrow. "Him," Cutter said, lifting his chin.

"Who?"

"The shell-game man."

Wojensky took another sidelong glance. A huckster in a green suit and green top hat was moving the three shells around on top of his folding table with great dexterity. A soldier thrust his tongue out in thought, tapped a shell tentatively, and the huckster lifted it. The pea was in a different shell, and the soldier moved on with a shrug as the huckster swept the coins from the table and dropped them into his pocket.

"What about him?"

Cutter Grimes said, "He's the man who used to run the roulette wheel at the Lucky Drover. The man who cleaned me out. I went back looking for him once," Cutter continued. He glanced at Wojensky admitting, "I think I might have killed him for taking my stake. I knew by then that I wasn't going to get out of the army and marry my gal at all. I also figured that he had cheated me. It had to be.

"But," Cutter shrugged, "he had moved on. Nobody knew where. I found out his name was Jack Wallace. That was all. I guess it was best. I had me a head full of whiskey and two Scoffs tucked into my belt."

Wojensky studied the man more closely. After a minute he had another sucker, and he shifted the shells while his line of patter drifted across the midway.

"I'll be back," Wojensky said. He sunk a hand into his pocket, finding his last five dollars.

"What are you going to do?"

"Test the waters. You stay here now, Cutter, hear? I don't want this gambling man making any connection."

Cutter's expression was blank, but he nodded, watching as Wojensky sauntered across the midway toward the green-clad shell-game operator. Another soldier lost two dollars. A sodbuster won fifty cents. A soldier lost a dollar.

"Who's next?" Jack Wallace asked. His was a toothy face, long and gaunt. "You?" His eyes fell on Wojensky. "You, Corporal?"

"I don't know."

Wojensky tilted his hat forward and scratched his neck. "Seems kinder difficult."

"Easy as pie." Wallace smiled. "Here's the little pea. I put it under the shell. Zip. Zip. Zap. Where is it?"

Hesitantly, Wojensky touched the shell on the left and Wallace peeked under it, revealing the pea.

"That's how it's done, Corporal. Of course, I'm a little quicker when there's money on the table."

"I'll bet," Wojensky said under his breath.

"How about it? Fifty cents. A dollar. A dime."

"What's the limit?" Wojensky asked.

"Why, no limit," Wallace said with an oily smile. "Whatever you can spare."

"I'm talking about *five* dollars," Wo said as if it were a thousand.

"Like I say, no limit."

"All right." Wojensky feigned reluctance and carefully put down his stack of silver dollars. "Do your damnedest."

"Here they go, watch them close," Wallace chattered. "The sharpest eyes will win the most." He stopped. "Choose your poison, Corporal."

Wojensky frowned, started to tap the one on the left, then switched to the middle shell.

"You sure?" Wallace asked.

"I'm sure," Wojensky said, turning to smile with confidence at the crowd.

Then Wallace tipped back the middle shell. No pea. "Sorry, you should have gone with your first instinct," he said, picking up the shell on the left. The pea rolled out from under it. Wallace swept up the money and went on to the next pigeon.

Wojensky walked away, shoulders bowed. He came up beside Cutter, took his arm, and led him away. "We've got him, Cutter," Wojensky said with a broad grin. "We've got that man nailed good."

"What do you mean?"

"Mean? I mean start packing your duffel, son. You'll be out and wandering back to that gal in West Virginia by this time tomorrow night, with a little luck. Just a little luck and three hundred dollars."

"That's always been the problem," Cutter said in exasperation. "Where in hell are we going to get three hundred dollars?"

"Why, from that man back there," Wojensky said. "Jack Wallace is going to give you back the money he took from you, if I've got anything to say about it. And I think I have." Cutter looked unimpressed, doom darkening his features. "Buck up, Cutter. The deed is practically done right now."

They met the rest of the boys coming back. Malone's uniform was torn, his face bruised, and he was grinning. Stretch Dobbs and Lumpy Torkleson were munching on candy corn from a big sack they shared. Holzer was not around, nor was Reb.

"Wait a few minutes," Wojensky said, glancing at his watch.

After another half hour, Reb McBride appeared. His walk was unsteady, his eyes seemed glazed. His mouth was open in a gaping, slack-jawed expression.

"He's drunker'n I am," Malone said.

But as he drew nearer they could see it wasn't alcohol. He was in some sort of a stupor, and they looked closely at him.

"Think he got hit on the head?" Stretch suggested.

Reb was smiling, leaning against Torkleson. "'S beautiful," he slurred. "M'M fine. Just . . . tired. 'M fine."

They walked him on toward the outpost. He seemed to be all right, only that stupid shit-eating grin just wouldn't come off his face.

Just as they were clearing the midway, Stretch happened

to glance toward the wagon to their right, and he gripped Wojensky's sleeve.

"Look."

Wojensky's head swiveled that way just in time to see Holzer disappearing behind the wagon with a woman in tow. A woman with a beard.

She was a big woman, but not overly heavy. She had a full bust and broad Nordic features, and a thick black beard.

"We'd better get him," Stretch insisted.

"Hell, leave him alone," Malone muttered. He and Reb were leaning against each other for support.

"Maybe he's having some fun," Wojensky said.

"He couldn't!" Stretch said. The idea was repulsive, incredible. A woman with a beard? "Nobody could."

"You never know," Reb drawled. Then he began giggling and could not be silenced.

Holzer had peered back around the corner of the wagon, his head appearing and disappearing. Obviously someone was tugging at his arm. Holzer grinned, pointing at himself and then at Wojensky.

Wojensky waved him back. "Stay for a while if you want," the squad leader told Holzer. Wolfie's face was blank. He squinted, trying to understand the English. "Stay here for a while if you want!" Wojensky repeated, cupping his hands to his mouth. "Stay. Here."

Holzer's face beamed and he nodded, was pulled off balance, and disappeared. Wojensky burst into laughter, as did Malone. Reb's giggling continued, and together they walked back toward the outpost, laughing and singing.

From time to time Stretch would look back over his shoulder, slap his thigh in disbelief, and say, "with a damned circus freak yet!"

That in turn would set off Reb's giggling, and they wound through the night, a noisy, hysterical little parade.

The quiet ones were flattened against the earth along the river bottom, a ground fog slipping past their watching, dark eyes.

The two young agency Cheyenne were called Tom Bull

106

and Walking Stick. They had seen some remarkable things emerge from the white man's seemingly limitless world. For their grandparents it had been iron pots, steel knives, guns, and glass beads.

The white man had brought machines that could sew, stringed boxes that sang, lamps of glass, the wheel, magic glasses that could see into the distance. Tom Bull and Walking Stick had heard of or seen houses of stone, locomotives, windows that you could see through but that stopped the winter wind.

But this was awesome. This mad, swirling, colorful, beeping, banging, jangling circus with women who danced on horses' backs, with great cougars that wore striped coats, a man who threw knives with a skill that even a Cheyenne would envy, men who flew from swinging ropes, who walked taut wires and juggled heavy clubs.

All of that was remarkable, but it was this other thing that defied belief, stunned the imagination, challenged the evidence of the eyes.

Gray, wrinkled, kindly, massive, and as tall as two ponies, it had the bulk of four bull buffalo and an elongated nose like a heavy rope, which could heft logs or take a small nut gently from the hand to be popped into its mouth.

The sign said it was called Jumbo. And Tom Bull and Walking Stick could only stare.

They had inched closer, scurrying up the river bottom, moving like shadows in the night. They had watched the man with the stick move the elephant around by tugging on its mammoth ear. They had watched it pick up handfuls of hay and dust itself with them. Once it bellowed. Amazingly, it lifted that trunk and trumpeted against the night, and the sound sent a chill up Tom Bull's spine.

Yet it appeared docile. It did not molest its keeper. And the idea had begun to grow in Tom Bull's mind.

"There. That creature."

Walking Stick was a year younger and a deal more cautious.

"It would be a great coup," he agreed. "But it could crush us, Tom."

"No." Tom Bull shrugged as if Walking Stick were be-

107

having like a child. "I have seen the man. I can make the creature walk beside me."

In his head a picture flashed. Tom Bull leading the great creature into camp, the children falling back in awe as he strutted, the old men slapping him on the back, telling him what a hunter he must be, not only to find such a creature, but to have tamed it.

He would tell a great tale of having ridden it across the plains until, exhausted, the creature bowed to his mastery. As they lay and watched it, the idea seemed inspired, and as they watched Walking Stick too began to have visions of grandeur. He had been trying to impress a beautiful girl called Kawina.

"You do not even have a rifle," she had scoffed, tossing her proud head. "How can you hope to have a woman of your own? You are not yet a hunter, but a boy with stick arrows, Walking Stick."

And what would she think if he and Tom Bull came into their camp astride this mighty animal?

"I think you are right, Tom," he said in a low voice. "We must count coup. We must take this creature."

ten

Reveille brought Malone up with a start. Then his head began to pound and he drooped back, holding his hand to his forehead. It was five minutes before he tried again. By then, Stretch was up and moving, and Cutter Grimes looked as if he hadn't been to bed at all. Torkleson was gone, and Reb was just returning from blowing reveille. Damned if he wasn't still grinning.

"Must've been something," Malone said somberly.

"I'll tell you when it looks like you can stand the excitement," Reb promised.

Wojensky stood in the doorway looking around, his eyes narrowed slightly.

"What's up?" Reb asked.

"Anybody seen Holzer?"

They looked at each other. "Not since last night," Malone answered.

"Damn. I think I got me an AWOL," Wojensky muttered.

"He's not AWOL," Reb said. "Hell, you know where he is."

"Where he *was*," Wo corrected. "I'm going to have to report him missing at muster."

"Come on, Wojensky!"

"It's his ass or mine."

"Might be yours anyway," Reb said softly. Wojensky was puzzled and Reb explained, "You told him to stay where he was. You know Wolfie's English. You told him to stay, he damn well stayed."

"Never thought of that. But I can't cover for a man who's AWOL."

This statement was met with contemptuous stares, and Wojensky relented. "Ah, shit, I'll try. Wolfie's going to

109

have him a fine, furry day, isn't he? I can't go in and pick him up until tonight."

"What's duty?" Grimes asked.

"Fire detail. But we're going to have to ride half a mile or so west. Everything toward the circus has been picked clean. Won't be able to slip over and get Holzer that way, but it was a good idea."

Malone picked up his gloves, muttering, "Just what I wanted to do today. Stoop down and pick up buffalo chips all day. With this head."

"Let's get some grub," Wojensky said. Reb glanced at his watch and walked out, his bugle in hand for grub call.

"Not me," Stretch said. "I can't take no more of Dutch's grub, either."

"Dutch ain't making breakfast," Wojensky said.

"You're kidding."

"Nope. He's flat on his back, says he's sick. Maybe he poisoned himself, I don't know, but Lumpy's making breakfast."

"Torkleson?" Malone turned sharply around. "Can he cook?"

"I don't know, but it couldn't get no worse, could it?"

Reb was blowing grub call and they went out the door, waiting a minute for Reb to catch up. Cutter followed with his habitual long face.

"Poor damn son of a bitch," Reb said, nodding at Cutter Grimes.

"Don't you worry about that," Wojensky said. "Daddy's going to take care of it." He thumped his own chest with a fist.

"You got something in the works?" Reb asked. "Really?"

"I got it nailed down, soldier."

"This I got to hear about," Reb said.

"I'll trade you." Reb was puzzled and Wojensky went on, "I'll tell you what I've got in mind right after you tell me just what went on with you last night."

"You'd think I was lying," Reb said.

"Will I think it's a good lie?"

"The best."

"Then I'll settle for that."

110

Breakfast was a feast. Oatmeal with brown sugar and butter melting on top, fresh eggs, ham on the side, crisp two-inch-thick toast, and rich coffee.

Wojensky spotted Torkleson through the serving door. "You're doing it right, Lumpy. Whatever you're doing, it's working."

Lumpy nodded, stacked a trayful of dishes in the sink, and called back, "Any of you all want some more, just holler."

"Did you here that? No cussin', no turnin' red in the face, no throwing things around. The man acts like a real, actual human being! Not like a cook at all." Reb smiled, tipped his chair back against the wall, and hooked his thumbs into his belt as he waited for his third cup of coffee to cool.

"You see, Wojensky? Everything's settling down. Life has its ups and downs. We've just been through one of those temporary little downs with Dutch and Cutter's problem and the hornies, and all. Now we are working on an up!" His hand described an "up" in the air and Wojensky smiled.

He would have felt better about this "up" if he had Wolfgang Holzer here to enjoy it with his squad instead of snuggling up in some circus wagon with a furry lady.

Ben Cohen was feeling "up" as well. He had just finished the best breakfast he'd had in weeks. He decided to stroll back and compliment Torkleson.

As he stepped into the kitchen, the first man he saw was Rothausen. Dutch looked up at him out of red eyes, his face that of a whipped, spiritless man.

"A KP, Ben. You let a KP take over my kitchen."

"I didn't have any choice, Dutch."

"Sure. I'm on my way out. What next? You know the last time I rode patrol, Ben? The last time I was on a horse? God!" He sagged forward, his head in his hands. Ben felt bad about it, but Dutch would get over it. He'd be back storming and cussing, throwing things around, and turning out the best meals west of the Mississippi. He just needed a little time to pull himself together. And in the meantime, why, Torkleson was a damned fine replacement.

Lumpy was scrubbing up some pots and Ben told him,

"Hell, you don't have to do that now, chef. That's what the KPs are for."

"Sergeant, this ain't right," Lumpy said quietly. "Sergeant Rothausen, he's liable to break my neck. You should see the way he looks at me, like a damned traitor."

"Don't worry about that," Cohen told him. "Just keep on doing good work. By the way—" He lifted a pot lid and asked, "What's for dinner?"

"That's another small thing," Lumpy told him, his big face knotted with concern. "I ain't sure."

"What do you mean?"

"Well, I'm not really a cook, you know."

"Don't downgrade yourself, son. You've cooked a dandy breakfast."

"Yeah? That's the trouble, Sergeant. You see, breakfast is all I can cook."

"What the hell are you talking about?"

"I mean that's all I ever cooked back home. Aunt Polly and them always made the dinner and supper. Soups, roasts, ribs—hell, I was always plumb awful at that. Used to burn everything up. Never got the hang of anything but eggs and ham."

Cohen took the big soldier by his shoulders. "You're shitting me, right, Torkleson?" His eyes searched Lumpy's. "That's it. You're shitting me. Tell me you are."

"I'm not, Sergeant Cohen. Why would I do that?"

"Damn!" Ben turned and walked to where Dutch Rothausen sat, hands pressed to his head, slumped on a sack of potatoes. "Dutch! Snap to it. This is still your kitchen. Get up and get with it."

"I can't, Ben."

"Get up, dammit! I'll break your sad face for you."

"My days are gone," Dutch moaned. "A KP can do anything I can do. Better." Then, to Cohen's astonishment, the big cook began to blubber. Ben drew back a hand, wanting to slap the man to life, but Dutch looked so damned miserable sitting there that it just wasn't possible. You don't kick a man when he's down.

"God dammit." Ben kicked the potato sack and stomped out. Now he had really blown it. Half a Dutch was better than a recruit KP who couldn't do a thing but fry eggs.

He nearly walked into Captain Conway on his way out the kitchen door.

"Morning, sir!" Ben said, louder than he had intended.

"You all right, Sergeant Cohen?"

"Fine, sir. Fine as frog's hair."

"I decided to stop in for breakfast this morning," Warner Conway explained. "It's been a while since I've eaten grub with the enlisted men. It was excellent. I just wanted to step in and tell Sergeant Rothausen that he hasn't slipped any."

The captain took a step forward and Ben Cohen blocked his way.

"Sergeant!"

"Were you going by, sir? Sorry, sir. Rothausen isn't in the kitchen right now," he lied. "He was seeing to his garbage detail, last I saw him."

For a minute Cohen thought Captain Conway was going to step by him, but then the officer shrugged and said, "Well, I'll have to catch up with him later. If you see him, Ben, make sure he knows I appreciate the job he's doing." He turned and added, "And I should say I appreciate your work, Ben. Like I tell everyone, you're the one who keeps the wheels oiled around here."

"Yes, sir. Thank you, sir. I'll tell Sergeant Rothausen that you extend your compliments and appreciation."

Warner Conway glanced at Ben Cohen. That strange formality in Ben's voice was usually a warning that something was rotten somewhere. But whatever was bothering Ben, it certainly wasn't going on in Rothausen's domain. He glanced out the door and told Cohen, "They're forming up, Ben. Better make sure we're all present and accounted for. Make sure nobody's run off with the circus," he joked.

"Yes, sir," Ben said with a hesitant smile. Conway looked at his first sergeant again, and then strode toward his office, his thoughts returning to Bates DeQueen.

With roll call over, Ben walked back to the orderly room, Rothausen still plaguing his thoughts. He had gambled and lost. He had pushed Rothausen over the brink. Now what?

He poured his coffee, drummed his fingers on the desk,

and pondered it, coming up with no solution. There was a rap at the door and Corporals Wojensky and McBride came in, both wearing that slide-away expression of someone with something unpleasant on his mind.

"Now what?" Ben grumbled. "You got that squad out on fire detail, Wojensky?"

"Yes, Sergeant Cohen," Wojensky answered formally, and Cohen was immediately on the alert. He knew, just as Captain Conway had in their conversation a few minutes earlier, that this respectful tone was a sure sign of trouble. Unlike Coway, however, Cohen was unwilling to let it pass.

"So what is it?" He looked from Reb to Wojensky and back again.

"We want to tap the slush fund," Reb finally said.

"Tap the . . . ? Is this about Cutter Grimes? I already told him there's not that much money, and if there was, I couldn't give it to him."

"It's for Cutter, but we only want to borrow the money, Sergeant Cohen," Wojensky said.

"*Borrow* it?" He shook his head. "And you two will pay it back? How? Besides, there's no three hundred dollars in there."

"We took up a little collection to cover the rest, Ben," Reb told him.

"We'll return the money tomorrow."

"Why don't you boys just sit down," Ben said, "and tell me what this is all about."

Wojensky told him, "It started back when Cutter was slickered out of his stake." He went through the whole plan, with Ben Cohen watching him silently, tight-lipped the entire time. When he was through, Ben said:

"And if it doesn't work, then the slush fund is dry, Grimes is still here, the men are out, and anybody else who needs money for a ticket home or help for his family is out of luck."

"It'll work," Wojensky said.

Ben looked again at Wojensky, intently, then at Reb. Finally, shaking his head in wonderment at his own gullibility, Ben reached into his drawer, removed the tin box, and slapped it on his desk.

"Go ahead. Clean it out."

"Thanks, Ben. Thanks a lot. You won't regret it."

"Take it. Go." He waved a hand.

After they were gone, Ben leaned back in his chair, eyes shut tightly for a minute. What did it matter if they lost it all? Ben had a notion that he himself was liable to end up on permanent KP. Things were falling apart, and there seemed to be nothing he could do about it. Thank God the captain was wrapped up in his own problems right now.

Bates DeQueen. And what a prize package he was.

Ben poured himself a second cup of coffee, sipped it, and then heard a shout. The gate was swinging open and Taylor's patrol was riding in. Dusty, haggard, but all the saddles were full.

Ben walked to the captain's door and tapped. Leaning in, he advised Conway, "Patrol coming in, sir. No casualties."

Taylor, accompanied by Windy Mandalian, tied up in front of the orderly room, dusted himself off, and, with the grizzled scout at his heels, stepped onto the porch to meet Ben Cohen, who saluted and then shook his hand.

"Rough one, sir?" Ben asked.

"Only dry and then too wet and then dry again, Sergeant," Taylor told him.

"Captain Conway's waiting for you."

Taylor went on in, still dusting himself off. "How's about something to eat?" Windy asked Ben.

"How about ham and eggs?"

"Cain't beat it," Windy replied, shucking the last of his chaw of cut-plug into Cohen's wastebasket.

"It all depends," Ben answered. Windy waited for an explanation, but he got none from Cohen. Together the two men walked to the mess hall.

Warner Conway rose as Lieutenant Taylor came in, and offered him a seat first and then a glass of whiskey from the bottle he kept in his desk drawer. Taylor took the whiskey with thanks and sipped at it. "No luck, sir," he said.

"What happened?"

Matt Kincaid had entered the room, and Warner Conway nodded. Taylor and Kincaid shook hands and Matt declined a glass of whiskey.

"We picked up a hot trail down along Sioux Falls, rode

115

north three days. Too late for a party of buffalo skinners. Elk Tooth hung them up and skinned them alive."

Taylor sighed, sipped at his drink, and then stood as he noticed a civilian in the room. Warner Conway introduced them.

"Mr. Taylor, Mr. DeQueen. Lieutenant Taylor has just returned from the field," Conway said. "I'll have to ask you to excuse us while the lieutenant gives his report."

"It surely can't hurt anything for me to sit in on this," Bates DeQueen said. "Do you think I'm going to run to the Cheyenne with military secrets?"

"It does not concern you, sir," Conway told him. "There is no headline in this, nothing to interest you. Please leave."

Taylor read the tension between the two men, and he glanced at Kincaid. Matt only shrugged. DeQueen turned on his heel. He left the room, tight-lipped and flushed.

"A newspaperman, did I understand you to say, sir?" Taylor asked after DeQueen was gone.

"Yes and a bullheaded damn fool newspaperman. He's out here searching for the truth of things, Taylor. Yet he's convinced, apparently, that what he sees and what he hears is fabricated to steer him away from our secret plots and machinations. He wants a conspiracy, a war, a drama so badly that he can't see that the unvarnished truth holds a fascination, and that he would be doing the entire nation, Indians included, a service by printing the flat truth." Conway poured himself a short drink, although it was still early. "I apologize. The man does have a way of annoying me." He nodded to Taylor. "Go on, please."

"We rode as far as Camas Meadows, then lost their tracks in the rain and sloughs. Windy guessed they would water at Camas, but we found no sign there. Probably Elk Tooth simply watered his ponies with the rainwater that settled in the buffalo wallows after that little storm the other night."

"Then you lost him completely."

"I regret to say we did, sir," Taylor admitted. "Windy thinks they may have circled back, drifted toward the mountains. If they have no fear of the Shoshone, and Elk Tooth never has indicated a fear of anything or anyone, it's possible they went on over the hump to winter on the western slopes."

"But you don't think so?" Conway asked his second lieutenant.

"No, sir." Taylor's eyes were cool, his jaw set. "I don't think so, but it's only an instinct, something I can't justify with facts. But I think the bloody son of a bitch has circled back and I think he'll raise bloody hell with us until winter shuts him down."

Bates DeQueen stood in front of the orderly room for a long while, watching the clouds scudding past against the azure sky. He was chafing against this army-imposed restraint. The War Department had promised the *New York Herald* full and complete cooperation. This was far from that.

He heard the ringing of a hammer from near the paddock. Someone shouted from the barracks. A work detail was resodding a corner of the roof near the front wall.

Then he saw her—squat, small, standing just outside the gate, waving frantically—and Bates DeQueen turned sharply away. The all-efficient army couldn't even keep that fat squaw from following him around!

He glanced back once, disgusted at the pathetic hope in her eyes. Quail Song watched him go, then sagged to the ground again, sitting heavily, patiently.

"You have an admirer," Flora Conway said as DeQueen strode past her door. "Would you like some coffee, Mr. DeQueen? Or some tea? I think I have a little tea in reserve."

DeQueen accepted. He liked this slender, graceful woman, and it was more for the sake of her intelligent conversation than for the coffee that he joined her in her parlor.

She smoothed her skirt and sat opposite DeQueen, sipping her coffee to test the temperature.

"That was a quick interview," Flora said.

"They, uh, gave me the boot," DeQueen answered sharply, then he smiled an apology; Mrs. Conway had nothing to do with it.

"I saw Mr. Taylor ride in, and I thought that might be the case," she answered mildly. "It's not personal," she assured him. "Warner doesn't like me or anyone else around when the officers are in conference."

"Apparently," DeQueen sniffed, "your husband is una-

117

ware of the First Amendment to the Constitution."

"I hardly think he is unaware of it," Flora answered, a bit more rigidly. "Warner Conway is a soldier, dear Mr. DeQueen. He cares first for his country, second for his command, and third for his wife. We do find ourselves in a state of war here, and as you know, war and censorship must coexist."

"I might agree," DeQueen replied, "if I could even be sure a state of war *does* exist. I understood that Sitting Bull has taken his Sioux across the Canadian border, and as for the Cheyenne locally, I have heard tales, but I have seen neither bloodshed nor mayhem. Heard no shots, seen no wounded."

"Then indeed you have been quite fortunate, dear Mr. DeQueen." Flora smiled sweetly, but her words were firm. "We have seen such things all too often. Maggie and I have cared for the wounded, bandaged them, at times helped as the surgeon—which is to say our cook, armed with a meat saw—amputated gangrenous limbs. You have missed much; you have been fortunate. Perhaps Warner simply does not take freedom of the press to mean the freedom of newspapermen to march themselves into hostile territory to be butchered."

"I see you have quite fallen into the spirit of things here, Mrs. Conway."

"You think I exaggerate?" Flora asked.

"I think you dramatize. I think it is important to your husband and to the War Department to invoke specters of Indian slaughter in order to encourage the allocation of funds."

"Do you really?" Flora asked, and there was a hint of mockery in the faint smile she wore. "Then I was wrong about you, sir. I thought you were merely ambitious, eager to discover the truth of things. I did not think you bigoted or foolish."

"No," DeQueen argued. "It's not that at all. I see now, you only want to make me appear foolish for wishing to leave this controlled little patch of reservation. Any suggestion that I speak with the other side has been ridiculed by each of you, your husband, Lieutenant Kincaid, yourself.

I see now, quite clearly, that you are afraid of the truth."

"No, Mr. DeQueen," Flora said, shaking her head a little sadly. "We are only afraid that you will find some way of getting yourself killed before you are safely out of the territory. My husband does wish to cooperate, believe me. But not to cooperate in your suicide."

None of that was convincing to DeQueen. He changed the subject, describing to Flora the newest fashions in the East, the Washington and New York gossip. Yet in a small, obstinate corner of his mind a plan was forming, nagging insistently at Bates DeQueen.

Back in his room in the visiting officers' quarters, he paced the floor. He was aware suddenly of the weight of the Schofield, Smith & Wesson pistol Matt Kincaid had given him, and he yanked it from his coat pocket, tossing it on his bunk.

You certainly don't talk peacefully to a man while you're carrying a gun. And that was exactly what Bates DeQueen had in mind now. He wanted to find some wild Indians. It was imperative, to his way of thinking, to have their side of it from their own lips. Otherwise he was returning with half a story, the official army line. *That* he could have gotten in Washington.

He was vaguely uneasy about actually doing this, but he could not believe the Indians would harm him. Why should they when he was a lone, unarmed man? Why should they, when he would make it clear that he had come to write their story for all America to read? You do not kill a man who has come to do you a service.

It was only a matter of biding his time now, of waiting for the proper moment. He paced the floor again, the idea building to a fever. It hit him suddenly. Now.

Now was the time. With Conway and Kincaid, his watchdog, in conference. There was nothing to it. Simply ride through the gate.

Hastily he gathered up his notebooks, stuffing them into his saddlebags. He picked up his canteen and sauntered to the door, where he paused to look around the empty parade. Smiling, he set off determinedly toward the stables, lugging his gear.

A few moments later he emerged, mounted, from the stables and walked his horse nonchalantly toward the gate. He waved to the gate guard, shouted something about seeing the circus, and rode past, turning that way. Quail Song rose to her feet, watching as her future husband rode past on that prancing, long-legged bay.

DeQueen ignored her, and when he had reached the stand of oaks along the wash, he turned sharply westward and kneed the bay into a gallop, riding out onto the empty, windswept plains as Outpost Number Nine gradually receded into the distance.

eleven ———————————

The high clouds held a sheen of gold and deep violet
at sundown. Warner Conway watched the darkening skies,
taking in a deep breath of clear, cold air. He noticed Matt
Kincaid near the visiting officers' barracks and he walked
that way.

"Evening, sir," Matt said. "Hell of a nice sundown."

Conway looked once again to the skies. He nodded.
"What's up with our guest, Matt?" He looked at DeQueen's
closed door.

"Sulking, I guess. The latch string's in. Thank God tomorrow's his last day."

"None too soon," Captain Conway agreed. "Then we
can just sit back and await the sentence, can't we, Matt?"

"You don't think there was quite enough 'positive image'?" Matt asked with a smile.

"I don't know." Warner Conway looked again at Bates
DeQueen's closed door. "Tell the truth, I'm not really sure
what is going on in his mind. Is he trying to rile us, see
what surfaces? Or is he dead set to pin something, anything,
on the army? He's a funny little man, maybe that's the way
he has to be—mistrusting, always looking for the dirt under
the carpet." Warner shook his head. "No sense in your
hanging around here, Matt. I'll post a man."

"I could use some grub," Matt said. "I haven't eaten
yet."

"I'll have Ben send someone over. Eat, Matt. Go over
to that damned circus if there's anything you haven't seen.
No sense in both of us worrying about Mr. DeQueen."

"All right. Thank you, sir."

Back to the circus. He had no business thinking of her,

121

but his mind had been on Carla Bramante all day. He could plainly see in his mind those long, tanned legs, that tempting, quite inviting smile. It couldn't hurt to wander on over.

A handful of enlisted men were already on their way. Mostly they were men who had been out with Taylor's patrol or stuck on duty last night, but there were a few repeaters, those who knew how to handle Ben Cohen and wangle a second pass.

Wojensky and Reb McBride, for instance. Matt smiled wryly. There was always something working with them. Surprisingly, Dutch Rothausen was ambling on over that way, but his head was hanging, and there was no enthusiasm on his broad face.

"Sir?" Private King was behind Matt, and he turned to salute. "Sergeant Cohen sent me over to relieve you."

"Yes. Just keep an eye on the civilian if and when he comes out, King. Likely now he'll sleep all night, but stand by anyway."

"Yes sir."

Matt glanced one last time at DeQueen's door, and for a moment he was uneasy, but he had a man posted and he had other things on his mind right now. Long-legged things.

Brassy, chanting calliope music drifted through the night, and Matt turned back toward his quarters, thinking that maybe another shave might be in order.

Reb, Cutter Grimes, Wojensky, and Lumpy Torkleson strode the midway, trying to look casual and carefree. But tonight they were here on business. Their eyes swept the circus grounds, searching for the man with the shell game. He was nowhere to be seen.

"Goddamn," Grimes moaned. "He's gone. I know it. He spotted me and took off."

"He's waiting for the big show to end," Wojensky guessed. "Then the midway will be filled with folks. That's when Jack Wallace will get to work."

"So?" Reb shrugged. "What'll we do till then?"

Wojensky saw a heavy shuffling figure coming their way from the western end of the midway, and a slow smile bent his mouth.

"That," he said.

122

Reb looked up to see the wide form of Dutch Rothausen striding toward them. "You got something working on him?"

Wojensky nodded. "What do you think?"

"Dutch ain't so bad," Lumpy objected. "You all should leave him alone."

"Son," Wojensky said, placing his hands on Lumpy's huge shoulders, "I sure would, but by God, when a man is trying to kill me, I got to fight back a little. And Dutch Rothausen is trying to do us all in."

"Stick to my plan," Malone said. He took a swig from his whiskey bottle and burped. "Get the man some ass."

"No." Wojensky reached for the bottle and helped himself to a drink. "My way's best. Get the man so damned mad he'll stop all the moping and get back to yelling at us. And cooking some good food."

"I don't want to be around when he blows his stack," Reb said honestly.

"I do. I want to see it." Wojensky nodded toward the Tower of Strength. "You just keep an eye on Dutch. When you see him heading that way, you keep your eyes open and stand by for an explosion."

Matt Kincaid searched the shadows before tapping on the wagon door. All his good sense told him he should let this one slide past, but his glands were doing a lot of arguing.

The door opened and Carla stood there, her dark hair loose around her shoulders, backlighted by the faint glow of a lantern. She wore a gold-colored wrapper, which she clutched shut, and her smile was a warm welcome.

"I was hoping you'd come back," she said. Her eyes sparkled with sensuality.

"I thought I should at least stop by and see that your friend wasn't bothering you."

"Arturo?"

"That was his name, wasn't it?"

"Yes. He has not bothered me. Won't you come in? I have coffee and some whiskey somewhere."

"You don't have a show to do?" Matt asked.

"No. The girl who usually does it, Gerta, she's well now."

"Maybe for a minute."

"Please," Carla said, and her liquid eyes were fixed on him.

"All right." Matt nodded and walked inside, feeling the brush of her hip against his thigh, smelling the sweet, soft fragrance of scented bath soap. He sat on the settee, placing his hat on the low table beside him as Carla went into the other compartment to get the whiskey.

Her hips swayed with fluid grace, consciously or unconsciously igniting Matt's interest. She returned in a moment, bending low to hand him his drink, the smooth contours of her breasts revealed by the parting wrapper.

She sat beside him, turning her face to him, her lips parted to reveal an even row of white teeth. Matt sipped at the whiskey and she said, "Why waste the time we have?"

He smiled at her. "No need to," he replied, and she rose and walked to the door, locking it.

Carla sat on the settee again, her legs folded under her, and kissed Matt Kincaid lightly on the neck, as her hand rested on his shoulder. He set the whiskey aside without finishing it.

He drew her to him and they kissed deeply once, then again, Carla's lips sucking at his, her hands gripping his shoulders.

Matt touched her cheek with the back of his hand and she nipped at his fingers with those fine, strong teeth. His hand slid across the base of her throat and beneath the silky fabric of her wrapper. He found her breast and cupped it, feeling the warmth, the womanly softness. Then his thumb flicked over her nipple and Carla's head lolled back as Matt loosened her robe and his lips went to her breasts, tendering a hundred tiny gentle kisses.

"You make me so hot, Matt," Carla said, as if from out of a swoon. "My blood, it pounds."

He kissed her moist, full lips, and her hand slowly unbuttoned his shirt. She toyed with the hair on his chest as Matt kissed her smooth neck and tongued the small pink ear he found beneath the gloss of her dark hair.

"I like that. Do you like me, Matt? My body is getting ready for you. Kiss me again. Here." She parted her gown

124

and held her breasts to him, and he suckled greedily as Carla petted his hair, purring as she guided him.

"You're so damned beautiful," Matt said. His eyes lifted to hers.

"You think so?"

"Of course."

"You tell me what you like best, " Carla said. She stood and, with her eyes half closed, let the silken wrapper rustle to the floor. She stood there splendidly nude, her eyes glittering.

"All of you," Matt said hoarsely. "I love every inch of you. What a magnificent creature."

"These?" Carla ran her hands up along her ribs and she cupped those full, firm breasts in her hands, offering them to Matt, who kissed them. Teasingly she pulled back.

"And from behind, Matt? Am I beautiful there too?"

She turned and he put his hands on the smooth contours of her hips, letting his thumbs drift into the crease between her buttocks. He kissed her there, first one side and then the other, and he told her, "Beautiful there too, Carla."

Matt's cock was swollen now, straining against his trousers. He felt a little dizzy, felt the blood rush to his groin.

"My legs, Matt?" Carla asked. "Beautiful to you?"

She stretched one long, lithe leg out and placed her heel on the arm of the settee, next to Matt. Then she leaned far forward, her long dark hair draping her thigh. Matt's hands ran up over the smooth, shapely calf, brushing the inside of her thigh. Through the veil of Carla's hair he could see the dark patch of hair between her thighs, the tiniest flash of pink.

His fingers crept toward it. Carla laughed and stood erect. "But you are a man, and that is what you find the most beautiful, eh, Matt?"

She smiled and sat on the carpet, her legs spread, and parted the bush that flourished there, opening herself to Matt's intense gaze. Now his pulse was positively racing. She spread herself, her hair veiling her face. Her index fingers dipped lazily into her cleft, and she stimulated herself as Matt watched.

She threw back her head, shaking the hair from her eyes,

arching her back. "I am full of heat. The honey of need, Matt. The need for you."

Still she touched herself, running a finger over her taut clitoris, and Matt trembled with excitement. Abruptly she stopped and stood, her eyes sparkling, her breathing deep, cadenced.

"And you, Matt. You are beautiful to me. If my woman's form excites you, your body sends thrills through me, causes me to tremble and drip juices. Come," she encouraged, "let me see you, Matt. Let me have the same pleasure."

She helped him as he stood. She unbuttoned two of his shirt buttons and kissed his chest, her lips going to his small, dark nipples. Then, as his fingers worked on the other buttons, her mouth followed them down to his belt, her kisses light against his hard abdomen.

Matt tossed his shirt aside and kicked off his boots. "Such shoulders," she said. "Such a chest." Carla sat on the settee, one lazy finger still within her cleft as Matt dropped his trousers and his huge erection sprang free.

"Ah," she breathed. "Bring it to me, let me see you. So pretty, so pink and proud."

Matt stepped that way, resting his hands on her shoulders as she handled his shaft, her breath against it. Then her hands went between his legs, running across his scrotum, now taut with readiness. He could feel a tiny, insistent throbbing in his loins now, as Carla reached far under and found his buttocks, clenching them as she drew him nearer, as her hair brushed the exquisitely sensitive head of his cock.

"Didn't you say something about not wanting to waste time, Carla?" Matt whispered.

"You are ready to slide it in me, to split me with joy?"

"What do you think?"

"I think yes. If you are as ready as I am." She stood and they held each other tightly for a moment, their naked bodies slick. Matt started to lean her back onto the settee, but Carla objected.

Her mind was breathy, low. "There's a way I like it. Do you mind?"

"Carla, right now I don't care if you want it between your toes."

126

She smiled and then lowered herself to the floor. She lay on her back, and then, very quickly and smoothly, she flipped her legs up and over, her toes on the rug as her back curled. She lay there looking up at Matt from between her legs, her ass thrust toward him, just above her eyes.

"Is that comfortable?" Matt asked.

"It will be in a minute." She beckoned to him and he got to his knees, straddling her head to position the head of his cock. Her hand came up to aid him. Matt glanced down and saw her smiling deeply, luxuriantly between his legs. He eased forward and sank into that deliciously smooth, wonderfully moist cleft.

Bent up double as she was, Carla could watch him entering her, and she thrilled to it. Matt eased his cock in. His balls dangled just above her eyes, and one solemn and smooth hand caressed him there.

Matt wriggled forward until he was sunk to the hilt, then slowly she began to move against him. He leaned forward and kissed her right buttock, then the left. His thumbs ran toward the warm cove where he throbbed against her, and dipped inside just a ways.

Carla's hand appeared below him, and she worked it against her own clitoris as her hips nodded and rolled, as her flesh trembled and filled with blood.

Matt encircled these hips with his arms, and he hugged her to him. He could feel light, encouraging touches on his balls, and then Carla's legs wrapped around him and she began quivering, shaking as if to drain him, trembling and thrusting, her hands, her lips, her body pleading with him to fill her, to split her, to spurt and throb and tremble along with her.

"Come on," she murmured. "A little more." She sighed and a spasm washed across her; he felt her tighten against his probing cock and swell, contract, and shiver as some dam within her burst and she rocked and tore at him, her hands on his buttocks, balls, and cock until Matt exploded with a color-bright climax that nearly caused him to faint.

It was a magnificent, furious rush to orgasm, a muffled explosion deep within her depths, a draining of his loins. He knelt there trembling, Carla's tongue lapping at his inner thighs as he spasmed within her, as her inner muscles worked against him, milking him dry.

"No more. Not this way," Matt panted and he withdrew, his head whirring.

She was flat on her back, hands clutching at him, legs spread and elevated. "Now, mm," she pleaded, "don't leave me empty. Come back."

Matt rolled on top of her, their scents heavy, mingled in the close quarters. He slid into her once again, her breasts against his chest, their lips meeting in a long, intricate kiss as Carla began to rise, to swell and sway beneath him. Her legs locked around his hips and Matt felt the blood pounding in his temples as he worked against her, his stomach muscles cramping, his mouth dry, his head filled with dizzy lights.

"More," she demanded, and he gave her more, driving his shaft home again and again. To Carla it seemed that he was raking her spine with his cock, touching all the loose bundles of highly charged nerve endings that lay hidden here, there, a little deeper, just inside, everywhere, and again the dam burst, trickles of sweet heat flowing from her as Matt's cadence increased. She felt his lips, his rough hands on her tender nipples, beneath her hips, drawing her more tightly against him until at last he came again, locking his mouth against hers as he collapsed against her softness, lying there on the floor of the circus wagon, his heart pounding wildly, his breath ragged, her hands searching, fondling, stroking, caressing his hot flesh as they clung together.

Outside, a slender, black-eyed man fingered the ugly knife he had in his belt. Arturo's mouth was a grim line, his eyes were murderous.

"No more," he vowed under his breath. "There will be no more of this, Carla." He drew his knife from his belt and crouched in the shadows. "Not with this blue-butt. He shall not live out the night."

Cutter Grimes had spotted him. True to Wojensky's prediction, Jack Wallace had appeared on the midway as the show in the big tent ended to a gust of applause, and the folks streamed out.

Wallace had yawned, scratched himself, and tilted his

top hat to a jaunty angle. Then he had set up his table, beginning his patter as the crowds drifted along the midway.

"Well," Cutter breathed to Wojensky who waited in the shadow of a tent. "Let's go."

"Not yet. Let him get comfortable and careless," Wojensky said. He put a hand on Cutter's arm. "Just be patient, man."

Reb squatted on his heels, saying nothing. The three of them stared from out of the shadows, watching as the shell game began, Jack Wallace's voice crackling across the midway.

Cutter was itchy, shifting position constantly. Malone had rolled a cigarette and he sat in a crouch next to Reb, slowly smoking, the red glow illuminating his battered features.

"When?" Cutter demanded after nearly an hour of watching.

"Right now," Wojensky said.

twelve   ═══════════

Wojensky drifted toward Jack Wallace's shell game. Reb joined him, standing casually aside. Cutter watched from the shadows, his pulse racing in his throat. It was do or die here. Either Wojensky pulled this off or, like it or not, Cutter Grimes was going to do another hitch while his woman waited at home in West Virginia.

"Keep your eye on the pea! It's not so hard, it's easy to see," Jack Wallace called out.

They watched as a sodbuster dropped seventy-five cents, a soldier a quarter. One old, gnarled man dropped a dime and went away mumbling and grumbling.

"Come on, boys, double your money," Jack Wallace encouraged them. He let the next man walk away with two bucks, mentally totaled his take, and set up for the next pigeon.

That was the trick of the trade—they had to see somebody win once in a while. Wojensky was near the table now, scratching his arm with that aw-shucks stance he had used long ago in Ohio when he had shilled for the carnival.

Jack Wallace's eyes swept the crowd and he settled on Wojensky. "Win a nickel, win a dime. Keep your eye on the pea all the time. How 'bout you, son?"

Wojensky looked elaborately bashful and shifted his feet.

"Come on, you look like a soldier with a sharp eye."

"I'm purty quick," Wojensky agreed.

"Give it a try, double your money," Jack Wallace said with a toothy smile. He frowned briefly, recognizing Wojensky from the previous night, but if he felt any reluctance it didn't show. Repeaters were no new thing to him. Often gamblers, even casual gamblers, will try to make up the next night what they lost the last.

Wojensky nodded. "All right."

"Step right up, then!" Wallace said, still smiling.

"What's the limit?" Wojensky asked as he had the night before. His heart skipped a little until Jack Wallace gave him the same answer.

"Why, no limit, son. Whatever you feel is right."

"Good." Wojensky pulled the wad of bills from his pants and stacked it on the table.

Wallace's eyes got as big and round as saucers.

"How much is that?"

"Three hundred dollars," Wojensky told him.

Wallace laughed and tried to slip out from under it. "That must be a year's wages for you, soldier."

"More," Wojensky allowed.

"I can't let you lose that."

"I might win," Wojensky said. "That's the gamble, ain't it? You said no limit."

"But I didn't think—" He wiped his face with a silk scarf. "Are you sure?"

"I'm sure. You said no limit."

They had collected quite a crowd now, and they began to razz the shell-game man. "You said no limit. Let the soldier play!"

Wallace looked around uncertainly. He was ringed by soldiers and sodbusters with rifles in their hands. It was something he wasn't going to be able to back out of. Jack Wallace looked at the corporal standing before him and smiled slowly. "Sure." After all, the day he couldn't flim-flam a hick, he'd better hang it up. "I'll match that, soldier."

He pulled a huge roll of bills out of his green silk hat and counted out three hundred.

"Have your try," he chanted. "The hand is quicker than the eye."

He flashed the pea, slipped it under a shell and began working, his patter continuing as he shifted and wove the shells. Then he stopped abruptly and smiled.

"Where's the pea, soldier?"

Cutter, standing back in the shadows, felt his heart turn over. Wojensky looked from one shell to the other.

"Well, it's not under this one," Wojensky said loudly, tapping the one on his right.

132

"No!" Wallace said in irritation. "Which one *is* it under, not which one *isn't* it under."

"Like I say, it ain't under this one." Wojensky flipped it over and Wallace looked like he was going to have a seizure.

"And," Wojensky went on, "I don't believe it's under the middle shell, either." Wojensky turned that shell over as well. Wallace watched him woodenly, the color drained out of his face.

"So it must be under that one," Wojensky smiled. He picked up the money and Wallace made a dive for it.

"Leave him be," an old, hunched-over farmer said. He was withered and dried and appeared all joints and rawhide, but he had steel in his voice and a rifle in his hands.

"He cheated!" Wallace screamed.

"How?" The old man rubbed his jaw. "It seems to me that sayin' where the pea *ain't* is just the same as tellin' you where it is."

There was a murmur of agreement from the crowd. Jack Wallace was immobile, his eyes slithering around from one face to the other. They were not going to let him get away with it.

"Take the goddamned money and shove it!" he said in exasperation.

"You shouldn't be like that about it," Wojensky said. Calmly then, he reached out and turned the other shell over. There was no pea there, either, and the crowd's murmur turned into an angry buzz.

Wojensky took Wallace's hand, opened it, and showed everyone the little green pea that nestled there. Wallace dropped it as if it were red hot. Wojensky touched his hatbrim and turned away, folding the money as the crowd surged forward, many of them demanding their money back. Wojensky heard the clatter of the table being knocked over, followed by a howl of pain, but he did not look back. He walked straight ahead to where Cutter Grimes stood with wobbly knees, watching him.

"That was something!" Reb clapped him on the back, and Malone broke into an impromptu jig. Wojensky handed the money to Cutter Grimes, who took it slowly, reverently.

"The fruits of a wasted youth," Wojensky said. Then he

133

told Cutter, "You stick that damned money away. You give it to Pop Evans tonight!" He grinned. "Then, by God, you pack your duffel and get your butt back to West Virginia!"

They walked back along the midway, laughing and congratulating each other. Jack Wallace had submerged into the milling mob. Malone had half a quart of whiskey left, and they drank that in two rounds. The night turned warmer now with the whiskey settling, especially for Cutter.

Wojensky suddenly drew up, his eyes bugged out. He lifted a finger shakily.

"Look!"

They let their eyes follow the pointing finger. Ben Cohen stood with his wife near the Tower of Strength. Reb glanced at Wojensky.

"So?"

"Come on, I've got a nasty feeling crawling up my spine."

Reb and Malone exchanged shrugs and they went along, Cutter trailing. Lumpy Torkleson was at the Tower and he hefted the mallet, bringing it down with all the weight of his massive back and shoulders behind it. The bell rang clearly and Lumpy smiled, accepting a cigar from the operator.

"Cost me six bits," Lumpy said, puffing, "but it's like you said, mister. It's all in the balance. Once you let me in on the trick, why, there ain't nothin' to it."

"How about you, sergeant?" the man in the striped coat asked, holding out the mallet.

"Thank you, no," Ben Cohen said. Maggie held his arm and shook her head negatively as well.

Wojensky and the others managed to arrive just at this point, and the Tower of Strength operator turned, flicked the ash from his cigar, and winked broadly at Wojensky, who shook his head furiously.

"What's the matter?" Reb wanted to know.

"It was a setup for Dutch Rothausen. I told the man to be on the lookout for a big sergeant. He thinks it's Cohen I wanted set up." Wojensky waved a hand, trying to catch his attention. He caught Ben Cohen's eye instead, and Cohen leveled a puzzled glance at Wojensky and Reb.

"Come on, Sergeant," the operator said. "You mean you're going to let this private show you up?"

"Show me up!" Ben puffed up a little, but Maggie kept her grip on his arm. "I don't have to ding-a-ling that bell to prove anything to my boys. They know damed well I can whip any one of them."

"Do something!" Reb whispered.

"If I break it up now, he'll suspect us," Wojensky answered. "Just what do you think will happen then?"

Reb sunk into a deep silence. Lumpy Torkleson was beside Cohen, and he didn't help matters any when he said, "That's right, mister. Sergeant Cohen don't have to prove anything. So what if he *couldn't* ding that little bell? Why, we'd still know he was bull-tough and bear-mean."

"Are you suggesting that I couldn't do it, Torkleson?" Ben Cohen demanded.

"No, Sergeant. Why, I'm just saying that if you couldn't, well, you know all the men still would respect you."

Cohen glanced around casually, only now noticing how many of his men were standing nearby.

"Well"—he shrugged—"of course I could, if I wanted to. I just don't believe in these little displays, sir," he told the operator.

"I understand," the little man said in a way that was more taunt than agreement.

"Sure, Sarge," Torkleson said.

Cohen glanced at the soldiers gathered around, and then at Maggie. "Hold my hat, darling, will you?" he said.

"You don't have to, Ben," she reminded him.

"It's nothing. A nickel?" He fished in his pocket. "Sure, I'll have a try at it."

The Tower operator winked again at Wojensky, and Wojensky covered his face with his hands. Malone was grinning, getting ready to enjoy it.

Ben approached the Tower carefully, the big mallet slung over his shoulder. He looked up its varicolored length to the bell gleaming at the top. He put the mallet head on the ground, spit on his hands, and smiled at Maggie. Then he cocked the mallet and, with a great *whumpf* of air from his lungs drove it down against the balance board.

The brass cylinder rode up to "Pantywaist" and slid back down as a roar of laughter erupted from the crowd of soldiers.

Cohen's face reddened and he smiled across his shoulder at Maggie, who was holding her breath, knowing Ben's temper.

"Better let me have another try," Cohen said. Casually he flipped the operator another nickel.

"Sure." The operator snatched the nickel out of the air and pocketed it.

Cohen wound up again, his face a study in concentration, his lips clenched, eyes bulging, He whipped the mallet through the air, and the brass cylinder snapped off the end of the teeterboard, flying up along the cable. Abruptly it stopped, somewhere between "Lightweight" and "Sissy."

The operator shook his head, and Wojensky groaned audibly. Torkleson tried to help.

"You see, Sergeant, you have to get your balance—"

"Shut up, Private!" Ben Cohen snarled. Maggie watched as Ben stripped off his tunic and handed it to her, rolling up his shirtsleeves.

"Ben, you don't have to do this," she whispered.

"I do *now*," he answered shortly.

The crowd of soldiers had grown. They knotted up around the Tower of Strength, peering over each other's shoulders, whispering and chuckling. Torkleson tried again. "If you'd like me to show you, Sergeant Cohen, just say so."

"Torkleson," Cohen said brittlely, "you can shut up now, or after I take this mallet to your head."

Torkleson backed away, looking like a rejected puppy.

"Another try?" the operator asked.

"Yeah," Ben growled. He was suspicious of this gimmick, but he had just seen Torkleson ring the damned bell. He threw another nickel to the operator. The man pushed his derby hat lower, puffed at his cigar, and leaned cross-legged against the tower.

Ben filled his lungs with deep breaths of the cold air, set his feet, tested his balance, and hefted the mallet for the third time. He closed his eyes in brief concentration, then flexed his arms, circling the mallet overhead.

136

He moved to the teeterboard, aware of the snickering and whispered comments all around him. His neck and face reddened still more and he winged the hammer through the air, slamming it down with all the strength in those big shoulders.

The cylinder lifted hopefully, like an arrow darting toward the brass bell above. Ben's eyes lighted. The cylinder zipped toward the bell, reached "Hercules," faltered, and stopped.

"I think your balance was a little better that time," the operator said. He had an insufferable smirk on his face. Ben glanced at Maggie, took a deep breath, and shook his head.

Maggie Cohen came to him. "Give me my coat," Ben said.

"Try it again, Ben," she whispered.

"What for?"

"Try it again, dearest. And have that little man stand on the other side."

"What are you talking about?"

"Just something I noticed. There's a little pedal near his foot. I guess folks wouldn't generally notice it. All their eyes would be on the bell."

"It's a fix!" Ben exploded.

"Shh." Maggie patted his arm. "Just try it. We'll see if it is."

"If it is, I swear to Christ—"

Maggie shushed him again, and grumbling and huffing, Ben went back to the Tower. "One more time, slim," Ben said. He handed him a nickel. "You stand over there."

"What for?" The operator's face fell. "I always stand here."

"Not this time. I'm going to swing real hard, you see. I'm afraid I might accidentally hit you if you don't move your butt over there! You do understand me, don't you?"

"Yes sir," the operator agreed hastily.

He moved away and Ben hefted the hammer. He drove it down and the bell rang clearly. He shot the operator a savage look, swung the hammer again, and rang the bell again.

"You shifty little bastard," Ben muttered.

He swung the mallet again, harder, and the bell quivered as the cylinder hit it. The soldiers around Cohen began to applaud, to cheer him on. Ben swung again. The cylinder chimed against the bell four times in rapid succession.

Ben glowered at the operator, then muscled up and really put his back into it, shivering the bell with a solid blow. Again he swung the mallet, as if he were driving steel, and yet again, his muscles warming to the task.

"Hey!" the operator protested, but Ben paid him no mind. He rang the bell again, and the whole structure trembled. Again. Three more times. Then he hit it a tremendous finishing blow and the cylinder snapped into the bell, tearing it from its bracket, and the bell and cylinder both dropped to the earth as Cohen swung around, throwing the mallet aside.

"Make a fool out of me, will you?" He started toward the operator and the little man ducked under someone's legs, circled the Tower, and broke into a run across the midway, with Ben Cohen pursuing him as the soldiers hooted and cheered.

Matt Kincaid heard the uproar, but he paid it no mind. She was snuggled against him, her ripe breasts pressed to his chest, her knee slung up over his thigh. Her breathing was soft and moist agaist his throat as he held her.

He moved slightly and she responded, her mouth rolling toward his in her semi-sleep.

Matt's hand ran down her shoulder. Then he traced her spine, finding the soft rise of her hips, and she sighed, the layer of muscles beneath her flesh rippling.

She rolled on top of Matt, her eyes appearing as two slivers of sparkling obsidian behind the slits of her eyelids.

She straddled him, reached back, and found his half-erect shaft. Bringing it to life, she slid down onto it, a little shudder of pleasure quaking her lithe, warm body.

Matt felt himself slip into her warmth. Carla sat up, still astride him, her buttocks warm against his thighs. She leaned forward, bracing herself by placing her hands beside his shoulders. Her long dark hair brushed his abdomen as she lifted herself an inch and then another, her eyes closed in concentration.

She lifted herself another inch, and leaning forward slightly, she could see the thick, heavily veined erection of Matt Kincaid sliding through her soft, dark bush, and it excited her.

Matt's back arched slightly, his buttocks tightened. Carla swayed back and forth, her hair softly caressing his chest. He reached out and took her breasts into his hands, and their eyes met. Carla smiled, tossed her head back, and began a more deliberate, longer stroking.

She worked that way for a few long, tantalizing minutes, and then the tension began to build within her. She lay her head against Matt's chest, kissing his neck, his ear, his throat, his mouth as her hips began a striving, savage lifting and falling.

"God!" she murmured, and Matt kissed her passionately, holding her to him.

She banged against him now, her hips rising far into the air, leaving only the head of his cock inside to be nibbled at by the soft flesh. Then she shuddered forward, and he was aware of the sweet juices flooding from her as she worked frantically against him with those fluid, hungry hips.

He fastened his hands on her buttocks, holding her against him so that she didn't lose it.

She sat up rigidly, suddenly, working her pelvis in tiny circles against him, and she trembled. Matt came with a rush, and Carla was not far behind, her frantic motion increasing, and she came again, and yet again, all the small climaxes rolling into one long golden wave that she rode as Matt tried to tear her open, to turn her inside out, to cleave her.

Exhausted, they lay still, her heart pounding against his, her fingers making tiny, spasmodic movements against his shoulders.

"I want you to stay. Tonight. I won't be here tomorrow, Matt. Stay with me tonight."

"I can't, you know that."

He touched her lips with his finger and she kissed it.

"They won't miss you. One night with Carla."

"They'll miss me," Matt promised her.

"I'll stay." She sat up, her eyes bright, her body glossed by the narrow beam of moonlight through the high window. "I'll stay with you."

"And do what? No, Carla. The circus is your home."

"I'll live in the bushes like a savage. Just to wait for you, to hold you at night."

"It would never work."

"No," she sighed, leaning back against him. "No, it would never work. I only hate to see the night pass, Matt Kincaid." She kissed his eyes, his nose. "You are much a man, and a very kind man."

"You are much a woman, Carla," he responded. "Very much."

They lay silently together, Matt stroking her back until the chill of night was too much against their cooling bodies. Carla rose to get a blanket, but when she returned, Matt had swung his legs to the side of the bed.

"An hour longer, a few minutes," she said, holding him.

He petted her soft dark hair. It was tempting, but it was growing late. He knew it and so did Carla.

"No, I'm sorry. You don't know how sorry I am to leave, but I must, Carla."

"Another time." She shrugged, drew back, smiled, and then turned away, hiding the moistness in her eyes, the beginnings of a tear. "Another time we will meet, Matt Kincaid, and we shall have weeks, months to know each other."

"Another time." He kissed her shoulder and then walked to the chair where his trousers and shirt lay. Slowly he dressed. Carla did not look at him as she made the bed, putting her wrapper on, covering her lovely white shoulders.

"Carla." He was dressed, watching her as she stood, arms folded beneath her breasts, looking at a shuttered window.

She turned back toward him, her eyes a little wild.

"Matt," she said, her voice strangely muted. "It was fine. I like you so much. But please, please leave now. No more words."

140

He was to her in three strides. He kissed her forehead, felt her stiffen and then begin to respond, and stiffen again. "Goodbye, Carla," he said.

His hands slid from her shoulders and he turned, walking to the door. He opened it and a blast of chill air met him. With wobbly legs he stepped to the hard earth and heard the door slam behind him. Matt took a deep breath and, without glancing back, strode away.

He saw Arturo Mercator standing directly before him as he dipped down to cross the dry riverbed. The man was smiling, his teeth white in the night.

Matt took another step forward, holding his hands out in a gesture of peace.

Then he heard the rush of footsteps behind him and felt iron-hard arms clamp around him. At the same instant a knife appeared in Mercator's hand, and the little man moved toward him in a lunging motion.

Matt made himself relax as the arms locked tighter around him, then he bent his knees and shifted his weight to one foot, turning his hips slightly as he did so. There was a grunt of surprise. His unseen assailant's arms loosened their grip as the man found himself unexpectedly off balance. Matt gripped the man's huge arms and dropped to one knee, and the fellow went hurtling over Matt's head. It was the circus strongman, still wearing his leopard-skin loincloth. The strongman flew toward Arturo, who sidestepped, and the strongman landed flat on his back on the hard ground, driving his breath out with a powerful *whoosh*.

Arturo now moved menacingly forward again, carrying his knife low. His hair was over his face, his moon-bright face savage, determined.

"This doesn't make any sense, Arturo," Matt said as they circled each other.

"It does to me," Arturo answered. His little black eyes were gleaming. The strong man had rolled onto his hands and knees and now he was puking.

Arturo moved in and Matt slapped his wrist away, sidestepping as he did so. The little man cut backhanded at Matt, but Kincaid managed to kick out and his boot caught Arturo on the lowest left-side rib. He cursed and swallowed his pain, coming in more cautiously now.

He didn't want to hurt him, Matt knew, Arturo wanted to kill. He held the knife loosely, blade turned up for a slashing, eviscerating cut.

"This is too much to pay for your pride," Matt said. "Let it drop."

"Go to hell," Arturo snarled.

The strongman was getting to his feet. Matt circled, timing it so that he reached the big man just as he came erect. Without shifting his gaze away from Arturo, Matt drove his forearm against the bridge of the strongman's nose. He blinked, sighed and sagged back.

"You'll have to do it on your own," Matt said.

He was angry now, tired of this, and he beckoned Mercator toward him. "Come on, Artie. Let's see what you're made of. No wonder Carla doesn't think you're much of a man."

Arturo's eyes widened with rage, and his passion got the better of him. Unthinking, wanting only to kill, he rushed at Matt, his knife arcing down, glinting in the moonlight.

Matt reached out, took Arturo by the wrist with one hand, and placed the other on his elbow, locking it. Then he spun and knelt, forcing the knife-wielder facedown on the ground. Bending Arturo's wrist back on itself, Matt deftly released the young man's grip on the knife, removed it from his hand, and threw it into the bushes.

"You must go through a lot of knives in a year, kid," he said.

"You son of a bitch, I'll kill you!" Arturo spat.

Still controlling Arturo's arm, Matt stepped around him and twisted the arm, flipping Arturo over onto his back. Then, straddling him, pinning his arms to the ground with his knees, Matt grabbed Arturo by the ears and slammed his skull against the packed earth. He kept this up until the young man's eyes began to grow dull and blank, then he told him how things were.

"You goddamned idiot! What's the matter with you? Can't you see what you've got? You've got a beautiful, hot-blooded woman who loves you."

"That's why she slept with you."

142

"To get you mad. You pushed her into it. You bully her, try to rough her up. You ought to crawl over to that damned wagon and beg her forgiveness. And you know what? She'd forgive you. She'd take you in, wipe your nose for you, and she'd marry you, give you babies. If you'd only stop this damned crazy pushing, this insane jealousy!"

Mercator lay utterly still beneath Matt, like a submissive dog. His puffy lips moved, but he made no sound. He tried again.

"You think so?" he asked, feebly hopeful.

"I'd bet on it. She just didn't like you acting like you owned her before you were even married. You pushed, Arturo, and she pushed back, the only way she knew."

"But you think she wants me?"

"Hell, kid, I'd bet a month's wages on it. Yes. She loves you."

"She loves me." A slow, smirky, stupid smile spread across Arturo's bruised face. "I'm crazy about her, you know. That's the only reason I wanted to hurt you," he apologized.

"Sure, kid."

Matt eased off, lifting his knees from Arturo's arms. The kid sat up, shook his head, and accepted Matt's helping hand as he came to his feet.

"You think so?" he asked. "You really think so?"

"Get on over there and find out," Matt answered with a smile. And he did. The strongman got to his feet heavily, glanced at Matt, and scurried off like a big whipped mutt. Matt wiped back his hair, found his hat, and stood watching as the door to Carla's wagon was opened, as Arturo blocked out the light. There was the sound of soft voices and then he went on in, the door closing again.

Then Matt heard the sounds of rushing feet and he turned to find Sergeant Cohen, Reb, Wojensky, and a dozen others running his way.

"What is it?" he called.

"Cheyenne," Ben Cohen panted. "They hit the circus."

thirteen

Matt Kincaid was instantly alert, all business. "How many Indians, Ben? Any shots fired? Anyone down?"

"No shots, sir," Cohen reported. "Small party, I guess. They shook up some of the folks pretty good. Made off with the elephant."

"The elephant!" Matt stared at Cohen, but it was obvious he hadn't been drinking.

"All right. Get back to post. Get mounted and bring my horse."

"Yes sir!" Cohen saluted. "Raise the alarm?"

"No." Matt mentally counted heads. "We've enough men. Just notify the OD so he'll know what's going on. Private Dobbs, get the rest of the men and have them return to post. Have the gate secured."

Stretch saluted and replied, "Yes sir," then went stilting off on those long legs.

"What do you think this is?" Cohen asked.

"I don't know. Let's find them and have a look. They're not going to run fast or hide well with Jumbo, Sergeant."

Cohen went legging it for the outpost, and Matt walked along with a group of soldiers. There was a flurry of activity from behind them as the circus went dark and wagon doors slammed shut.

Ben was quicker than Matt would have guessed. He hadn't walked a quarter of a mile before Cohen was back, leading his horse. Matt stepped into the saddle of the bay, caught the gunbelt Ben tossed him, and they swung westward, tracking by the clear light of the early-rising moon.

"Didn't bother Windy," Ben told him as they rode. "He's beat, and I figure if we can't track an elephant on the plains,

145

we'd better just close down the post and go home."

Matt grunted an answer. It was growing cold, the horses blowing steam. The huge, nearly round footprints of Jumbo were sunk deep into the sod. "How many you make, Ben?" Matt asked.

"Only two of them, sir," Cohen replied. "Moving slow."

"They'd have to be."

It was comedic, of course. Yet if these two young bucks were part of Elk Tooth's group, it could turn serious suddenly. There were two now, but how many over the next rise?

"They're heading for the agency," Ben opined.

Matt nodded agreement. So there was nothing to this but a prank. But the fools could very easily have gotten themselves shot to rags. There were plenty of sodbusters walking that midway with rifles and shotguns. Many of them had been burned out or seen their families dead. Under those circumstances it doesn't take much to make a man trigger-happy.

Now Ben stood in his stirrups and pointed southward. A great, ambling silhouette plodded along the skyline.

Matt waved his arm. The patrol spread into a wide, nearly straight line as they closed the gap. They had their weapons at the ready. Too often, something that looked harmless had turned into a death trap.

They were within a hundred yards before the Cheyenne suddenly saw them and broke and ran.

"Gather them up," Matt shouted, and Cohen and Torkleson spurred on ahead. Cohen swooped down on Walking Stick and plucked him from the earth, holding him with his huge left arm as the kid kicked and waved frantic arms.

Torkleson had a different way of doing it. He propelled himself from the saddle, landing with a grunt and a cloud of dust as he flattened Tom Bull. He stood, holding the agency Indian by the arm as Matt rode up.

The kids had stopped struggling; they knew it was useless now. Matt stepped down and walked to them, identifying them.

"Ben, take three men and deliver them to Tom Weatherby. He'll be able to deal with this a lot better than we can."

146

And he would. Tom Weatherby loved these people, but he was firm with them. He had to be. An Indian who stole from the agency was ostracized. These boys would be cut off from any special treats, and so would their families. That would encourage the tribal elders themselves to discipline Tom Bull and Walking Stick, and they would.

Wojensky walked toward them, leading the elephant, and Matt Kincaid laughed. "You got a handle on that creature, Corporal?"

"Looks like." He patted its trunk. "I think she likes me, sir."

"Good. Then you can deliver her back to the circus. Take Torkleson along in case you have to wrestle her."

Matt swung back, leading the rest of the patrol to Outpost Number Nine. It had been quite a day, and that bunk was going to feel good. The sentries had been doubled and the gate was still locked. He heard men saddling up and collecting their gear, and saw a light on in Captain Conway's quarters.

"Damn it, I told Ben not to wake Conway."

"He didn't, sir," Malone interjected. "I was with the sergeant. He handled it just the way you told him to."

Matt frowned. Then something else was up. He kneed the bay forward, the gate opening before them. Taylor was up and dressed, and Windy Mandalian was standing beside him outside the captain's quarters as Matt swung down."

"Back so soon?" Taylor asked.

"It was only a couple of kids," Matt replied. Taylor's face was concerned. "What is it?"

"Hell, I thought you went out after him. DeQueen's gone, Matt. The guard got to wondering after he stood there a few hours hearing nothing, seeing no light in DeQueen's window. He reported to me and I had a look. He's gone, taken his notebooks and little else. His pistol was lying on his bunk."

Warner Conway, looking pale and drawn in the lantern light, emerged from his quarters. "No luck?" he asked Matt.

"Not with DeQueen. I just heard about that."

"I don't know where that fool has gone," Conway said, his voice taut. "But if there's any chance he could find Elk Tooth or any other hostiles . . . get out there, Matt. Take

147

Windy and get riding now. We've got to find that silly son of a bitch."

It was after ten o'clock when they rode out. There was no quessing where DeQueen would go; it was doubtful whether he knew himself. This was a straight tracking job, but Windy was up to it. As long as the moonlight held, they were able to ride at a pace only slightly slower than that of Bates DeQueen.

The trouble, of course, was that that was not fast enough. DeQueen gained ground with each mile. The Rockies, which had been invisible below the dark horizon, now jutted up starkly—black, massive, low silhouettes against the starlit sky.

They had crossed Turkey Creek and nearly reached Dirty Tanks. Matt was vaguely hopeful that DeQueen would remember there was water there and camp for the night.

No such luck. He had skirted the tanks and headed on towards the foothills. Windy pulled up abruptly and Matt rode toward the scout. Windy was down out of the saddle, and he looked up at Matt with concern etched into his dark features.

"Trouble, Matt. I make six unshod ponies crossing DeQueen's sign." He pointed with a gnarled finger. "They pulled up here, then turned west, riding in his tracks. He's going to have some company, and it likely won't be hospitable folks."

"Elk Tooth?"

"Can't say for sure." Windy dusted his hands as he stood. "But I was tracking that cuss all of last week, and I could almost swear I seen this toed-in print before. This horse was with Elk Tooth's band."

They rode more quickly after that. The clouds had begun to drift in and the moon skittered along behind them. Once, Windy lost the track and they circled back. The Indian ponies, in longer stride now, were still following DeQueen.

The clouds closed out the sky now, and they slowed to a walk. They were nearly past the slumped, unmoving figure beside the trail before they saw it.

Windy held up a hand and Matt saw it at the same time. He swung down quickly and walked to it. *DeQueen, dead?*

148

It wasn't. Quail Song lay huddled against the earth, her face streaked with the dusty tracks of tears, her shoulders rolling and shuddering with her sobs.

"She hurt?" Windy asked.

"I don't think so. Quail Song?" Matt said loudly. "Sit up! What happened?"

She bawled and snuffled and finally got her bulk into a sitting position. Her moccasins were worn clear through to her dark, chubby feet.

"My man. He ride away, and I follow. Then I see Cheyenne riders and I hide. I try to go on, but I cannot. Too tired. My man!" She wailed, and Matt had to back away from the piercing cry.

"We'll find him," Matt promised. That stilled her somewhat, but the blubbering continued. "Go back to the outpost, Quail Song."

She looked at him, shaking her head miserably.

"Tell her, Windy, and make it plain."

Windy spoke in Cheyenne, his words abrasive and threatening, and she just stared at him. Finally she struggled to her feet and turned eastward, her hunched figure disappearing into the night.

Windy chuckled and Matt asked, "What did you tell her?"

"I told her if she didn't get her butt movin' it was sure as hell going to be a long, cold winter. Told her you'd fix it so she didn't get no agency food nor nothing from the outpost. That was about the worst threat I could come up with."

It was dark and blustery. The skies were roofed over with drifting black clouds. There was no chance of tracking even a buffalo herd under these conditions, and so they dismounted, holding the reins of their horses as they waited for the first gleaming of dawn. If they were lucky, DeQueen might still be alive to see that dawn.

Dawn was a sharp, sudden rush of color against the eastern horizon, soon muted and swallowed up by the gray clouds. Bates De Queen rubbed his jaw where a stubble of beard now grew.

He hadn't seen smoke or fire, horsemen or horse any-

149

where on the broad, empty plains, and he was beginning to think there weren't even any Indians out here. Then he heard a faint, muffled sound and his head spun around. Six painted, heavily armed Cheyenne sat within fifty feet of him, the wind raking their ponies' manes, flattening the feathers knotted into their hair.

DeQueen flinched momentarily, then his smile broadened. He had found them. He stepped from the saddle and walked toward the renegade Cheyenne, positively beaming.

"Hello. Hello, there. Elk Tooth's men, are you? I've come to interview Elk Tooth for the newspapers. Appreciate it if you'd escort me to your camp."

Curly Wolf sat his paint pony beside War Eagle. The two older braves glanced at each other. They had their faces painted for war. They held Spencer carbines in their bronzed hands. Each man had a Colt revolver and a hatchet on his belt. Fresh scalps were knotted into the manes of their ponies.

Yet this man would confront them. What sense was there in that? Who was he? One of the young warriors, Crow Talk, leaped from his horse and, with a piercing war scream, rushed at DeQueen.

Quickly, War Eagle called Crow Talk off. The young brave walked around DeQueen in a circle, his hatchet dangling from his hand, his haughty head thrown back.

"What are you doing?" DeQueen inquired. "Oh, looking me over for weapons? I have none, you see." He held his coat open and smiled. "See, you have nothing to fear from me."

Curly Wolf and War Eagle exchanged rapid comments.

"This man is a crazy one."

"Or very brave. He has no weapon. He is alone." War Eagle respected that.

Curly Wolf was more inclined to believe Bates DeQueen was crazy. He shouted to DeQueen, holding up a raw scalp for him to see.

"Yes, very nice pelt," Bates called, waving a hand. He did not recognize it for what it was. He walked to Curly Wolf's horse and took the scalp. Turning it over, he asked, "Otter, is it? Or muskrat? I'm not very good with that sort of thing."

150

He handed the scalp back to Curly Wolf, wiped his hand fastidiously on his scarf, and stood, arms akimbo, grinning.

"Now then—I'd like to see Elk Tooth."

"Crazy," Curly Wolf said. The wind drifted his dark hair into his eyes. "He must not be harmed. A spirit lives in him."

"No, he is very brave," War Eagle still believed. "I do not see crazy eyes. He stands there inviting us to kill him. But there is no honor in killing a man like this."

"I'll kill him," Crow Talk said excitedly. The young warrior was returning with no coups counted, no scalps to boast on over the long, coming winter. He wanted DeQueen's hair.

"No," War Eagle said finally. He glanced at DeQueen, whose merry face bobbed up and down in happy anticipation. "Come with me, man," War Eagle said. "I will take you to Elk Tooth. He will decide."

Bates DeQueen was so excited he had trouble mounting. He rode with the "noble savages," grinning and chattering. He was especially taken with the young, handsome brave named Crow Talk, and he rode beside him all the way to Elk Tooth's camp.

With the sunrise, Windy was able to read the tracks across the plains like a map. They stretched the horses out into a gallop, every eye wary as they rode deeper into Elk Tooth's stronghold.

It was midmorning before Windy spun his buckskin around and rode in a tight circle. Then he stepped down. Matt walked his bay to the scout."

"They got him, Matt," Windy said.

Matt breathed a low curse. The sign was evident enough. Six or seven horses and DeQueen's horse. DeQueen's footprints. Matt looked around, eyes searching the grass and low brush.

"He ain't here. They didn't kill him," Windy said.

"Why not?"

"Couldn't say," Windy admitted. "But they didn't. Look. He got down, talked to them. Then they all rode off together. No signs of a struggle. No blood. Maybe," Windy suggested, "they took him back for the squaws to work over.

If so, I pity the poor son of a bitch."

"Ride at the ready," Matt told his patrol. "Let's track 'em home, Windy."

The scout frowned, his dark eyebrows arching. Then he stood, spat a stream of tobacco juice, and stepped into leather, leading off.

Matt rode silently. The wind was cold off the far mountains. He blamed himself for this, for the bloodshed that might follow. He should have kept closer tabs on DeQueen, though he knew he could have done little more. Yet there would be no excuse when this got back to Washington. It would likely be the end of the line for his career and Captain Conway's as well.

Oh, they would not court-martial them, or at least Matt doubted it. But it would hit the papers and that would be the end of the promotions. Permanent first lieutenant. Windy had halted, and now he raised his rifle over his head, signaling hostile contact.

The scout slid from the saddle, and Matt dismounted as well. Creeping up beside Windy, he could see the camp in the distance.

"Jesus," Matt said under his breath.

They had been tracking a half-dozen ponies. They had guessed Elk Tooth's strength at about a hundred braves, from Taylor's report. Nestled there along the river bottom were nearly two hundred tipis.

"We'd best get our butts out of here," Windy said.

"DeQueen's down there."

"Yes. And we'll all be down there, hanging from someone's lance, if we make any kind of a try at him. You know that, Matt. Excuse me if I'm speakin' out of turn, but they'll cut us to dog meat. We've got to back off, and now. Let the captain decide if he wants to hit this camp with all we've got. We sure ain't going to accomplish a thing but suicide with this patrol."

"If they have DeQueen—"

"I don't hear him," Windy said. He was right. If they were torturing DeQueen, it would be a slow job, plenty of fun for the squaws and kids. He would be screaming a long time. Until his voice gave out.

The scout told Matt, "Maybe they figured he was a heap brave man. You said he had no gun. Maybe they figured he was a crazy man—I go along with that idea my own self. Either way, the Cheyenne would be careful about killing him. Once you're in a Cheyenne camp, or any Indian's camp, you're treated well until you leave, even if you're the enemy. It's just simple good manners, you know that, Matt."

"I know it, Windy, but it scares the hell out of me, having that little man down there with Elk Tooth." Matt sighed, thought it over, and decided Windy was right. The odds were good that nothing would happen to DeQueen now. Besides, there was nothing they could do to help him. Through sheer stupidity the newspaperman had ridden into the hostile camp.

And it seemed that sheer stupidity was the only thing that kept him alive this far. *If* he was alive. Matt pulled his patrol back half a mile to a good position on a low knoll with some scrub oak cover, and sent a rider to Outpost Nine.

Then there was nothing to do but wait. Wait for the killing time.

fourteen _____

It was chilly along the river bottom. The rising bluffs, studded with scattered, wind-gnarled pines, kept the wind swirling, shrieking. Bates DeQueen sat with his new-found friend, Crow Talk, awaiting his interview. Crow Talk, DeQueen noted, was utterly fascinated with this white man. He touched his hair frequently and smiled at Bates.

Finally, War Eagle returned and Bates stood, dusting himself off. "Elk Tooth will see me?"

"You come." War Eagle was expressionless. He turned, and Bates DeQueen scampered after him.

The largest tipi belonged to Elk Tooth and Bates De-Queen pulled the flap aside and went in. The air was heavy and stale inside the tipi. Elk Tooth was alone in the tent. A broad-shouldered man with a deep chest, he was naked from the waist up. His features were finer than Bates had expected. Intelligent, black eyes, a dominant nose. He wore a chain of silver around his neck. A sort of star, or sun-symbol with long rays, dangled from the chain.

"Sit," Elk Tooth said without inflection. He watched as DeQueen did so, producing a notebook from his inner coat pocket.

Elk Tooth sat across from DeQueen on the blanket. No pipe was offered. "So you are from the newspaper in Washington."

"New York," DeQueen corrected, but Elk Tooth shrugged. All those distant villages were the same in his mind.

"You wish to write Elk Tooth's legend?"

"Why, yes. That would be one way of putting it. I do wish to write your legend so that all the people in the East will know of you and your exploits."

155

Elk Tooth nodded passively. "Yes." He waved a hand. "Ask what you like, and write that Elk Tooth has said it."

"Fine." DeQueen settled, his notebook on his knee as Elk Tooth stared at him. "I'd like to find out what has caused this conflict, and if and how the army has abused you to make you take up the lance instead of settling down near the agency."

"You ask too many questions," Elk Tooth said, stopping him.

"All right. First, then, why are we at war?"

Elk Tooth shrugged. "There is always war. From my grandfather's time, before. Always war. There is war because the white man is here and we are here. Before the white man came, we fought the Blackfoot, the Shoshone. No difference. Before the white man came here, he fought other white men. No difference."

"You act unconcerned," Bates commented.

Elk Tooth shrugged again. "Always there is war."

"But if the army would leave you alone, perhaps there would not be war. Do you hate the army, the soldiers? Do you know Conway?" DeQueen asked. "How do you feel about him? Bloodthirsty, is he?"

"Conway." Elk Tooth was thoughtful. "Brave man. Very good warrior. And also Kincaid. Brave men."

"You say that as if you respect them."

"They are men," Elk Tooth said.

"But the Indian agents are your friends. The soldiers wish to kill you!" DeQueen said in exasperation.

"Yes." Elk Tooth struggled to find the words he wanted. "Conway will fight me, kill me. When he says, 'I will fight you, Elk Tooth,' I know he means it. We understand each other. If he said, 'I will not fight you, Elk Tooth,' I would know Conway spoke the truth.

"But the agency—they say, 'We give you blankets, food.' No food comes. They say, 'You may live here.' Then a man comes and says, 'Move to the other side of the river.' We do not believe them, no matter what they say. We do not respect them! And so we use them and laugh in their faces. They give me guns and say, 'Promise you will fight no more,' and I promise and laugh and fight. Because they are not honorable, I am not honorable with them."

"This is incredible," DeQueen said. "You would prefer to deal with the army, a soldier like Conway, than the Agency?"

"Of course. If Conway says we fight, we will fight. If Conway says there is peace, there is peace. If he says he will give me presents, he will; if he says he will try to kill me, he will. Because he is a man! There is no man in the agency.

"A man says, 'I will give you this, Elk Tooth,' and then some time later he returns, very sad face, and says Washington will not give presents. 'Washington has not sent meat this winter, sorry.' They are not men. They are"—he frowned—"dolls on the string?"

"Puppets?"

"Yes." Elk Tooth spat. "Puppets."

"Frankly, I don't understand what you want, then, Elk Tooth. I assume you must—you have to—want peace."

"What for?" He leveled that dark gaze on Bates DeQueen. "Do I want to hoe corn, guard sheep, and wait for Washington to send me blankets when it's cold? When Washington says move here, I will move. Then Elk Tooth is a puppet! No, I will ride the plains. I will fight. I will die one day, and that will be that. But my legend will not say, 'Elk Tooth was a puppet.'"

Bates DeQueen was silent for a long while. He shook his head very heavily and said, "Frankly, I cannot understand your attitude."

"No?" Elk Tooth stood abruptly. "Then perhaps it is because you are not a man like Elk Tooth, a man like Conway. Maybe you are a man like the Washington man. If so, we cannot talk. Nothing will make sense. I do not wish my legend to be written by you," Elk Tooth decided. "It would not be true. Go now. Go while you can, and if you again see Elk Tooth, out on the plains, run, newspaperman. Run as fast as you can, as far as you can."

It was fading to darkness, the grass flattened before the rising wind. The clouds were mottled with shifting purples and deep reds. Matt Kincaid saw him first—a lone, slow-riding man, his shoulders hunched against the wind—and rode out to meet him.

"Hello, Lieutenant," Bates DeQueen said.

"You've given us some trouble, sir," Matt said.

"Yes. I expect I have." Then he fell into a thoughtful silence. He was that way through the entire trip back to the outpost. They met with Conway's force a mile out and swung back, reaching the gate as darkness fell.

Warner Conway had held back, checking his anger. Now, finally he asked, "What did you learn, Mr. DeQueen? What was worth the risk of your life and hundreds of others?"

"Learn?" Bates DeQueen glanced at Conway out of the shadow of his hatbrim. "Nothing, sir. I was puzzled for a time, but now I have it figured out. Elk Tooth—another sham. Another tame Indian, regurgitating the army line on cue. No, sir, I have not learned anything. Congratulations, Captain Conway, your scheme to let me speak to Elk Tooth worked to perfection. Now I see that he was not a hostile at all. You simply let me find him, hoping I might believe he was."

Matt Kincaid was furious. "If you can believe that—!"

Warner Conway silenced him, placing a hand on Matt's arm. "Leave him alone, Matt. After all, it's as he says—he didn't learn anything. And," he added quietly, "he never will."

Wojensky stepped down, stretching his back, and Reb dismounted beside him. They loosened their saddle cinches and looked to the skies.

"Damn fine night," Wojensky said.

"You're right. It's a damn fine night to be alive. I wasn't sure there for a time."

"Quiet, ain't it?" Wojensky said as they led their horses toward the paddock. He glanced toward the circus grounds. The wagons had been packed and Milo Grimaldi had led them out, rolling on toward Montana. "Goddamn!" Wojensky suddenly stopped, stiffening. He turned toward Reb, his mouth open.

"What?"

"You don't think—? He couldn't have."

158

Then Reb got it and he whirled around, looking northward.

"Holzer!"

"I told him to stay put. Dammit, I told him to stay put.
In the wagon with the furry lady."

They found Ben Cohen and explained it to him, flattening
their ears for the chewing-out they got. It was a roar of bull-
moose proportions, but there was only one conclusion to
be reached, and Ben told them.

"Get your butts out there, find that damned circus, and
get that man back on this post! Now!"

They practically fell over each other, trying to get through
the door at the same time. Wojensky forgot he had loosened
his saddle cinch, and nearly fell off his horse. With a good
deal of cursing, Wojensky tightened his saddle and they
mounted on the run, riding through the gate and out into
the darkened plains, streaking northward.

Five miles out, they saw the campfires and slowed the
horses to a walk. The circus was drawn up in a loose circle
and they had no trouble finding Holzer.

Wojensky rapped with his boot on the side of the covered
wagon, and Holzer's head appeared.

"Hello, boys."

"Hello."

A second head appeared—a bright-eyed, giggly woman
with a black, curly beard—and Wojensky wiped a hand
across his eyes wearily.

"I haf stayed," Holzer said with a smile.

There was no point in yelling. Wojensky simply shook
his head. "It's time to go now," he told Holzer.

"Ach, *ja*. I was wonder."

"Don't go," the bearded lady squealed. Then she turned
his face to hers and planted a whiskered, wet kiss on his
lips. "Don't go, Wolfie!"

Holzer straightened himself heroically and said, "*Ja*. It
is duty!" he waved an emphatic finger in the air and accepted
Reb's hand as he swung up behind.

The bearded lady hung out of the wagon, bawling, her
arms outstretched as they turned the horses and headed back
across the dark and empty plains. From time to time Holzer

159

would turn and holler back forlornly, "Goodbye. Goodbye!"

Wojensky ground his teeth together and suggested that Holzer perform anatomical impossibilities, but Reb started to laugh and the laughter was infectious. They laughed long and hard, the tears streaming from their eyes as Wolfgang Holzer, arms crossed imperiously, sat straight-faced behind Reb McBride.

Outpost Number Nine was dead silent when they rode in, and Holzer hopped down, striding toward the barracks, unaware yet that he had done anything irregular.

"Coffee?" Reb suggested.

There was a light burning low in the mess hall, and the odds were that Dutch Rothausen had brewed a few gallons, anticipating a returning, weary patrol.

"Sure," Wojensky agreed. They walked to the mess hall, Reb still giggling intermittently. The door was open and they walked on in.

Reb stopped suddenly. "What's that?" he whispered.

Wojensky listened. There was a muffled whooshing sound, then a little squeal. Wojensky followed Reb, and they crept toward the kitchen.

Reb poked his head in and then withdrew, holding Wojensky by the shoulders. Reb's shoulders were rolling with silent laughter, and Wojensky had a look.

They looked like two sacks of potatoes on the floor. Dutch Rothausen's pants were down around his ankles, his flaccid white ass rolling and pushing. Quail Song lay beneath him, munching happily on a doughnut as Rothausen poked her, her eyes deeply contented, little mews of satisfaction rising from her throat.

Reb put his hand on Wojensky's shoulder and they eased out, letting the door close silently behind them.

"She must have got one look at him," Reb said outside, "found out what he did, and decided Dutch Rothausen was the man most likely to make it through a hard winter."

"May they enjoy," Wojensky said wearily.

It was late and chilly, and they tumbled into their bunks, where they slept peacefully until reveille.

fifteen ———————————

Wojensky rolled out with a sleepy yawn and pulled his boots on. Cutter Grimes was already up, and had been since four o'clock. He was polished and pressed, shaved and shorn. He had his duffel in his hands and a grin on his face.

"So this is it, huh?" Wojensky asked, putting out a hand.

"This is it. Last wake-up, last breakfast. Thanks to you, Wo. I can't ever thank you."

"Hell," Wojensky grumbled, "you just did."

Reb came in looking tired but cheerful. "That was grub call, boys. What about it?"

They walked on over to the mess hall, and even before they had gotten inside, they heard the roaring and cussing.

"You people that are finished, get your butts out of here! Goddammit, KP! I told you to wipe up that coffee! Can't you idiots do anything right!"

Wojensky just stood in shocked silence. It was Lumpy Torkleson who was raving. He turned toward them, and a sheepish smile spread across his face.

"You sure have turned around," Reb said. "Rothausen getting on you?"

"Naw. He's a swell fella, you know that?" Lumpy's voice dropped to a confidential whisper. "Guess what? As soon as they can swing it, they're going to reassign me. Put me into cooks' school. That's why I'm rantin' and a-cussin'. Sergeant Rothausen said you just have to get the hang of that!"

He turned then and shouted into the kitchen, "Those goddamned pots are stacking up pretty high! Let's get with it, knotheads!" Then he ambled off.

"Well," Reb said, "there's one we lost." Then he grinned.

Wojensky stood there in astonishment for a moment, then followed Reb to the table, where Malone was finishing up his coffee.

"At least Torkleson won't be here," Wojensky said. "And our mess sergeant is nice and quieted down now."

He tried his egg, nodded, and sipped the coffee. Breakfast was fresh, hot, and well cooked. The kitchen door burst open suddenly and a KP came tumbling through it. In a second Dutch Rothausen appeared, fists clenched, face red.

"How many times I got to tell you idiots! Toast the toast, don't incinerate it!"

"Nice and quiet," Reb said. Wojensky shuddered.

"Don't worry about it, boys," Malone said, leaning back with a toothpick in his teeth. "How you like that breakfast?"

"Fine. And I figure I better enjoy it, if Torkleson's leaving," Wojensky said.

"Dutch cooked this morning," Malone told them. "And you can smell that buffalo stew he's fixing for dinner." Malone leaned across the table and winked. "You boys ought to pay more attention to my theories. I hear he's got a stubby little Indian gal hanging around now. Everything's going to be fine, boys." A crash from the kitchen interrupted him and Malone sighed, "Normal, anyway."

They stood on the parade watching as Gus McCrae rolled his Concord stage in and pulled up. A new recruit stepped down, and they saw Ben Cohen heading for the fresh meat.

Cutter Grimes was shaking hands all around, and they went over to give him a final goodbye. Then he stepped up into the box next to Gus and waved, and the coach turned, rolling eastward.

Cohen had the new man by the ear and was reading him the book. "Welcome to Easy Company. If you keep your ears open and your mouth shut, you'll find us firm but fair . . ."

Cutter waved his arm one last time and then was gone. Reb sat down on the porch next to Wojensky and Malone. "Well, he's gone home. One in and one out. Nothing much changes, does it?"

"Oh, it's changing all the time," Wojensky answered.

"The main thing is to learn from what happens."

"Some never do," Malone said. He looked toward the vanishing stage, where the rigid, tight-lipped face of Bates DeQueen was still visible for a moment.

"Wonder what the hell he's going to write about us when he gets back to New York?"

"No tellin'. You can be sure of one thing, it'll be just a little slanted, just a little twisted. A man like that, he can't stand to have everything square and straight forward. To the end of his days he'll probably believe there was some kind of conspiracy out here."

Malone stood and stretched, and Wojensky got to his feet as well, tugging his hat low against the sun. The clouds had drifted away and the breeze was light.

"Nice day, isn't it?" Wojensky said. "Makes a man feel like doing something useful. I believe I'll wander out and collect some buffalo chips. Either of you gentlemen care to come along?"

"Might as well," Malone said. "It'll keep us out of trouble."

"I'd better come along too," Reb said. "There's an art to it, and you boys have been slipping lately. What you've got to do is make sure they're not too big, nor too little. A thick one may look like a find, but I favor them about saucer-size, with just a little..."

The dust from the Concord sifted through the air and settled. It was silent across the parade, except for the voice of Ben Cohen:

"I am Sergeant Cohen and I am the first soldier, When I say froggy, I expect you to jump. If you think you can whip me, I'll be glad to take off my stripes and show you the error of your ways...."

one ───────────────

Crystal-clear water, crisp and fresh, gurgled in the sparkling sunlight as it wound along the course of the stream known as Cole Creek, named after the homesteader who had been found lying facedown in its upper origins many years before. His scalp had been taken and a Sioux war arrow, with its unmistakable yellow and red stripes, was lodged between his shoulder blades. His hat had drifted downstream, flowing with the meandering stream bed on the High Plains waterway in Montana Territory, and the place where it had been found, lodged against the bank, had come to be known as Lost Hat Crossing.

Six riders sat their mounts at that crossing now, while their horses nuzzled the icy water, and they were a hard-looking gang of men. Colt revolvers hung from their narrow hips, stocks of Winchesters protruded from their saddle scabbards, and stock ropes hung in coiled loops from their saddlehorns.

The eldest man, and obviously their leader, had a stern but strangely appealing ruggedness about him. In his early fifties, John Cole wore his years well, even though his swarthy face was weather-creased from years of exposure to wind and sun. A full but neatly tended mustache was prominent on his upper lip, and its gray coloring matched the long sideburns visible beneath a wide-brimmed Stetson hat. A fur-lined jacket covered his broad shoulders, and there was a wiry leanness about him that bespoke a lifetime of hard labor. But it was the eyes that were the most prominent thing about him as he stared into the meandering stream bed. Azure blue, they had a cold depth to them, the deep look of bitterness and heartbreaking loss, the look of

167

a man who had loved once in his lifetime, but who would never love again.

The man beside him, Jason Cole, was nearly an exact replica of his father, sans mustache and gray hair. At twenty years of age, hard years on the plains had left no mark on him, and the youthful vitality in his tanned face contrasted sharply with the rigid determination of the older man. Jason watched his father in silence and there was a look of deep compassion in his eyes as John Cole slowly removed his hat and held it by his side.

"You can't ever come here without remembering her, can you, Pa?" Jason said softly.

The elder Cole's thick, whitish-gray hair was brilliant in the strong morning sunlight, and he continued to stare down as though he had not heard what his son had said. Finally he spoke without looking up, and his words were muted, as if being uttered over the grave of a loved one.

"No I can't, son. Your ma was the most beautiful woman in the world and I loved her more than anything I've ever known, before or since. I still can't believe she's dead."

"It's been eighteen years now, Pa. You're going to have to get over her sometime."

"No, don't think so. You were only two years old when we lost her, so I can understand how you might forget. But—"

"I didn't say I forgot, Pa. What I meant was, it's time to accept the fact that Ma's never coming back to us."

John Cole slowly replaced his hat, tore his eyes from the stream bed, and stared upriver. "Eighteen years ago your grandpa was killed by the Sioux. We know that 'cause his body was found. I had taken you and your sister into Garderville with me for supplies, 'cause both you little tykes loved to ride up on the seat of the wagon with me. When we got back home your ma was gone, the homestead burned down, and all the stock killed. No trace of your ma has ever been seen since that time."

Cole paused, rubbing an old knee injury with one hand and remembering the past. "I rebuilt the place in your ma's memory. Everything is just the way it was when I last saw her. And someday I'll find her and bring her home and it'll

168

be just like she'd never left. Maybe like she was coming downstairs from a nap or something."

"If she wasn't killed, Pa, she was taken by the Sioux," Jason said gently. "She could never live with them for eighteen years."

"She was a strong-willed woman, your ma. If there was a way to survive, she'd find it. Just like I have, even when they put that Sioux reservation next to my land. God knows how I hate them, but I've learned to live with it."

Jason studied the stream bed. "It's a little ironic, isn't it, the government using Cole Creek as the boundary between our property and the reservation?"

"Yes it is. I didn't like it, but there wasn't anything I could do about it. This stream is our life's blood. That's why your grandpa and me chose this place. Without the water we get from this creek for our stock, the Grace Land spread, which I named after your ma, would be just another piece of useless prairie soil. That old creek there cuts through our ground, then into the reservation, runs along here, forming a boundary, and then back into our place again. Even though I don't wish them well of any kind, Cole Creek here helps the Sioux just as much as it does us. And they need it just as bad."

"Well, they've never given us any trouble over it in the past, so maybe it's one thing we can share. Just as long as they stay on their side and we stay on ours, this water's free for anybody to use."

"I'm aware of that. That's why I come here every so often, to make sure—"

"John? Look over yonder," said a hired hand named Mike Reeves, raising his gloved hand and pointing to the northwest. "Looks like about twenty of 'em to me."

Cole's eyes snapped in the direction indicated, and the hard look instantly returned to his face. A band of Sioux warriors sat their ponies on the crest of a prairie swell at a distance of possibly a hundred yards. They were uniformly dressed in moccasins, tanned leggings, and vests; feathers dangled from their braided black hair. Each had a rifle across his lap, and there was a stoic silence about them, as if they had been frozen in time and were more painting or a sculpture than living, breathing human beings.

Even though hatred instantly boiled in Cole's heart, he couldn't help but admire how magnificently wild and fierce the Sioux looked, and they reminded him of a herd of splendid antelope, swift and free.

"Son of bitches," he said under his breath. "Don't anybody move. I've never seen them this close to our ground before. If they want a fight, we'll give 'em one, but let them make the first move."

The two sides stared at each other in silence, separated only by the lush growth of greasy grass shifting in rhythm with the wafting breeze. The only alien sound was the drifting cry of a prairie falcon, shrieking primeval rage at a target missed. A minute, then two, elapsed before a lone warrior moved forward and walked his mount down the hill at a leisurely, almost unconcerned pace. They could see he was fairly young, possibly twenty, but his countenance was that of a man who had fought many battles and to whom the humility of defeat was an unknown phenomenon. When he stopped his horse at the edge of the stream, which was twenty yards wide at the crossing, a ragged scar was visible across his chest and exposed through the open buckskin vest. There was an air of nonchalant pride about the Sioux warrior, but his lean body was taut and poised like a man prepared to leap suddenly away from some danger yet unseen. He held his rifle in his right hand and gripped the hackamore in his left, jerking the pony's head up and denying it a drink of the water coursing past its hooves. He looked at the white men across from him with unflinching eyes and spoke in a controlled tone:

"Hear me! I am Black Eagle, chief of the Lakota. I will meet one of you at the middle of the stream. I have words that you must hear."

Jason immediately lifted his reins, then pulled his horse back at a gesture from his father. "You stay here, son. I'll go. If anything happens, put a bullet through his brain for your ma."

Urging his horse into the stream, Cole spoke as the animal moved toward the center of the creek through fetlock-deep water. "My name is John Cole. I own the Grace Land spread and every damned head of cattle on it."

The Indian had matched Cole's move, and they stopped their horses at midstream, with the animals' heads not five feet apart. There was absolute silence between them as they stared evenly at one another while water gurgled around their horses' hooves. Finally, Cole spoke with bitter, contempt-encrusted words.

"You said you wanted to talk to me. I'm here. Let's get on with it."

The warrior's lips curled into a sneer and he nodded toward the far bank. "Why do they send one so old? Is the young one afraid of a Lakota warrior?"

"No, he's not afraid," Cole replied. "He's just not used to the putrid smell of bear grease. Say your piece."

"Peace? The white man says that word so easily. And always with the same result. You have taken Lakota land. And now you would take Lakota Minni as well."

"Minni?" Cole asked, genuinely confused. "I don't know what the hell you're talking about."

Black Eagle gestured downward with his rifle barrel. "Wakan Tonka has given this to us. No white man will take it away."

Cole glanced down and then back at the Sioux. "You mean water?"

"That's what I mean."

"Hell, boy, we don't want your water. This stream belongs to all of us, and nobody can take it away. Not me and not you."

"You are wrong. The Lakota do not wish to take it away from you. But you white men will take it away from us, like the flat-tailed one with the teeth."

Again, Cole was confused. "Do you mean beaver? Like a beaver dam?"

Black Eagle nodded, and there was hot contempt in his eyes. "*Heya.* You call them beaver. There were many, like buffalo, until the white man came."

"So what's this about a dam?" Cole asked, tiring of the confrontation.

171

"And you know nothing of it?"

"Not a goddamned thing."

"It is known that you hate the Lakota. I believe you wish to take our water. The big chief in Wa-sha-tung will listen to you. He sends white men here to take our Minni."

Cole's eyes narrowed as he studied the young warrior, trying to figure out the meaning of his words. "What the hell are you talking about, boy?"

"Without Minni-Tonka we will have no game to hunt. We will be slaves of the agency, waiting for food that never comes." Black Eagle's chest swelled and he squared his shoulders. "The Lakota will make war first."

"Don't be rattlin' your saber too loud in my direction, son. If it's war you want, it's war you'll get. Now what the hell is all this bullshit about a dam? I don't want this creek dammed up any more than you do. I haven't talked to anybody in Washington about it, but I damned sure will if one is built. What say you knock off the bragging about making war and try to talk a little sense?"

A contemptuous sneer curled around Black Eagle's lips. "The white man talks with two tongues and you are no different. In the direction from which the darkness comes, where the Minni-Tonka cuts deep into the earth, they build this dam of yours. They are the men with the hairy ears, and they are many."

Cole fell silent, studying the Indian's words. He knew "the men with the hairy ears" was a reference to the Army Corps' of Engineers, and he assumed the place where they were building was the one called Ryan's Ravine, which would be the only logical place for a dam. It was roughly a two-hour ride east from Lost Hat Crossing, and Cole felt a sense of dread fill his heart. If they actually were starting to build a dam, as it appeared they were, he knew it must be for some long-range purpose that could in no way be beneficial to his interest. Dams meant civilization, and civilization meant people. People equated to more homesteads and the loss of the federal land upon which he now had permits to graze his cattle. Not to mention the increased demands on an already limited water supply and tighter government control, which Cole hated even more than he did the Sioux. He had been watching the young warrior during the fleeting seconds it had taken for these thoughts to race through his mind, and now he lifted his reins, pulled his horse's head up, and prepared to turn away.

"Have you anything else to say to me?" he asked.

"*Heya.* If the Minni is taken away from us, all whites will die. I have spoken."

The two men stared at each other in extended silence, and Cole noticed a strange, disturbingly familiar look about the Sioux's eyes. Then he turned the horse toward the opposite bank.

"Spare me your threats, Black Eagle, or whoever in hell you are. You and your people won't be dealing with an old man and an unarmed woman this time. We're ready any time you are."

He heard the clatter of hooves on rock behind him, and the splashing sounds of a horse running through water, and he knew the warrior was galloping his mount from the stream bed. Cole reined in before his son and turned to watch the band of Sioux vanish on the far side of the rolling prairie swell.

"What was that all about, Pa?" Jason Cole asked.

Cole turned to look at his son. "Two things, mostly. That young buck there says he's going to kill all of us. And it seems the damned fool government is going to dam up Cole Creek."

"Dam it up? Why?"

"Well, me and that lad didn't get into specifics, but for whatever reason it is, I'm not likin' it. Let's ride on over to Ryan's Ravine and have a look for ourselves. Any dams built on this creek will be built over my dead body."

Major Brian Sacke rose from the cot in his tent and studied his image in a hand-held mirror. Even though he was thirty-five years of age, he had not had much luck with the side-burns that had earned his branch of the service the appellation of "hairy ears," and he thought he looked just slightly ridiculous with his thick-lensed, gold-rimmed glasses and sparse blond mustache. But he hoped the addition of the moustache and traditional hairstyle would give him a degree of much-needed respect from the men of his command and provide an air of authority. At six feet tall, with a lean, sparsely built frame, Sacke was aware of his nickname— "beanpole with windows"—and even though it was never uttered in his presence, it still rankled on him.

At the sound of approaching footsteps, he quickly shoved the mirror under his cot and assumed an authoritative position at the field desk on one side of the command tent.

"Major Sacke?" a voice demanded while the tent flap was thrown aside, and it was obvious the visitor had no intention of observing military courtesy.

Sacke turned to see the tall, rugged-looking captain who was five years his senior. "Yes, Captain Edgerton? What is it?"

"Where the hell's that mounted infantry unit that was supposed to be sent here to protect my men?"

Sacke noticed the customary lack of deference to rank, and he brushed his fledgling mustache with a nervous motion. "They should arrive any day now, Captain," he said, striving for an authoritative, confident tone and failing. "Is there some sort of problem?"

"Not now, Major, but there damned well might be. A band of about twenty featherheads was watching the timber detail this morning. Every damned one of 'em had a rifle, and the men said there was no questioning but that they were prepared to use them. Their leader, a young buck with a scar across his chest, damned near trampled Private Swanson when they rode away. I won't put up with that kind of shit, Major. We were sent here to build a dam, and even though this is a piss-poor place for one, that's just what we'll do."

There had long been a feeling of animosity between the Captain and Major Sacke. Call it jealousy of rank, pure contempt, or absolute lack of respect, but whatever it was, the major had always tried to keep as much distance between them as possible and, in so doing, hide his fear of Edgerton. Sacke cleared his throat unnecessarily.

"Well, ah, Captain, I certainly won't have my men harassed," he said, remembering that he had forgotten to send a telegram notifying Captain Conway at Outpost Number of his arrival at Garderville. "I'll send another telegram immediately and tell that infantry captain to get his ass and his troops up here on the double. As you know, I'm not one to mince words when a direct order is disobeyed."

The captain smiled coldly. "No, I'm sure you're not. And I'm not one to have my men double-crossed. Personally, I hate the sight of a blue-leg, or anybody else who can't handle a plumb line, but it sounds to me like those Sioux were just part of a bigger war party, and I haven't got time to kick the shit out of them and stay on schedule too."

"No, that's true. We have a job to do and we weren't sent out here to fight."

"Hell, there's nothing I like better than a good scrap, Major. But there's a time and place for everything. My boys and I always seem to find time to squeeze in a little brawl along the way."

Without saluting, the captain spun on his heel and stalked away. Sacke watched him go, wondering how he had ever wound up in a roughneck outfit like a field unit of the Army Corps of Engineers. Sure, he allowed as he watched the vacant doorway, it was true he had earned an engineering degree in college, and it was equally true that he had experienced no desire to be assigned to a combat unit when he'd joined the army. But he had envisioned a staff position in planning and management back in Washington, where the cut of his uniform would turn the ladies' heads and the dirt would be under someone else's fingernails. Such a position had been his until that fateful night when he had been caught in the bedroom of the daughter of the senator from Delaware.

Everything had gone to hell for him after that, Sacke remembered, absently tapping a pencil on the desktop. He had been shipped out West to locate, survey, and initiate construction on several proposed dams. The Garderville dam was to be the first, and the major had been less than enthusiastic upon selecting the site and settling in under what were, to him, barbaric living conditions to wait out the construction process. What the hell, he had thought when he packed his transom away that final time nearly a month before, out in this godforsaken land, a dam's a dam.

Major Sacke rose dejectedly, peeked through the tent flap, then turned and produced a flask of whiskey from a lower drawer and poured generously into a glass. He sighed as the glass moved toward his lips and mumbled to himself, "God, but I dread the long ride back into that fleabitten hole they call a town." He downed half the drink and blinked a film of moisture from his eyes. "What the hell is a man like me doing in a shithole like Garderville? It wouldn't even make a decent slum back in Wash—"

"Major Sacke?" came a hard voice from outside the tent, which the major immediately recognized as that of First Sergeant Fred Hatcher. Hatcher was a burly man, scarred from countless fights, and one who seemed to tolerate the major strictly through military necessity. "There's somebody out here to see you."

"Just—just a minute, Sergeant," Sacke replied, hastily downing the remainder of the whiskey, wiping his lips, and replacing the bottle in the drawer. "I'll be right out!"

Sacke straightened, adjusted his uniform, belched discreetly, and then marched toward the tent flap like a man propelled through great motivation. As he stepped into the sunlight he adjusted his hat and looked up at the six mounted range hands staring down at him.

"Major, this man here calls himself John Cole," Hatcher said, pointing a blunt finger at the lead rider. "He don't seem to be too fond of our little project here. You talk to him. I've got work to do," the sergeant concluded, moving off toward the ravine.

Major Sacke stepped forward with a somewhat nervous smile and offered his hand upward. "Good afternoon, sir. I am Major Brian Sacke, battalion commander. What can I do for you?"

Cole hesitated, watching the major's face for long moments before finally accepting the handshake.

"Like your man there said, I'm John Cole. I own a cattle spread about ten miles from here." Cole spoke in a slow but emphatic voice and folded his hands across the saddlehorn while staring at Sacke with cold, hard eyes. "My cows sometimes get a terrible fondness for water, and they're

176

used to drinkin' when the urge strikes them."

"So? What has that to do with me, Mr. Cole?"

Cole looked toward the ravine, where soldiers with picks and shovels were already preparing the escarpment of the dam, and then his attention shifted to another crew that was busily digging a ditch at an oblique angle to the northwest. After his gaze drifted over the men felling timber on the distant horizon, he looked again at Sacke.

"Everything," he said flatly. "Whose decision was it to build a dam here?"

Sacke cleared his throat and adjusted his glasses. "Well, I guess it was mine, sir. I selected the site and am in complete charge of construction."

"Then you're the idiot that I want to talk to."

"That's fairly strong language, Mr. Cole. I'm sure you intend to explain."

"You're damned right I do. Obviously some of your men are digging a channel over there to divert the water, isn't that right?"

"That is correct. There is a natural stream bed just over that rise—"

"And that one isn't?" Cole snapped, jabbing a finger toward Cole Creek.

"Please let me continue, Mr. Cole. That other natural stream bed," Sacke said with the pride of great knowledge, "is utilized only during the winter rains. On its boundaries lie some of the best land with farming potential in this area, if only water could be provided year 'round. Which it will be, once this dam is completed."

"Farming land!" Cole boomed. "Hell, boy, this is cattle country, and there ain't been a plow stuck in the ground yet!"

"It is the intention of the United States Government to see that that oversight is corrected," Sacke said cautiously.

"And it is the intention of John Cole to see that it isn't. My pappy died to build a homestead for his family here, and I'll damned sure die to see that it isn't taken away."

"No one is talking of taking your homestead away, Mr. Cole."

"Like hell you're not! Do you know the course of that

'natural streambed,' as you call it?"

"Certainly I do. I have mapped and charted all the land in this area." Sacke turned slightly and gestured toward the tent. "Would you care to see the maps?"

"I don't need to see any maps, boy. I was ridin' over this ground when you were still just a twinkle in your daddy's eye. I know every inch of it, every buffalo wallow, prairie dog town, and water hole." The stockman's eyes narrowed as he said the last words. "And I also know that Cole Creek is the only reliable source of water in this entire goddamned area."

"Precisely why it was selected for damming, sir, and if you don't mind my saying so, I think you're getting a bit overexcited."

"Overexcited, your ass! When you were making your fancy maps and charts, did you happen to notice where that other stream bed crosses my property?"

Sacke hesitated. "Well, I didn't actually visit the location, but from the natural direction of travel, through geological necessity, I'd say it would have to cross somewhere near the northeast corner."

"The *extreme* northeast corner, young feller. As she runs now, Cole Creek provides a natural boundary between my ground and the Sioux reservation. My cattle very rarely cross, 'cause the graze is just as good on my side as on the other. They just go back the way they came. Cattle are creatures of habit, Major, and if that stream isn't where they found it, they'll cross onto the Sioux reservation and I'm gonna have myself a war with a young buck named Black Eagle. That's the long of it. The short is, I've got just as much right to that water as anybody else, if not more."

"And your rights will not be impinged upon, Mr. Cole. As you just stated, the new stream will *cross* your property," Sacke said with a weak smile.

"At a point where it won't do me any more damned good than trying to fill a bucket with a spoon. And that's a little job I don't plan to take on."

"Well, I'm terribly sorry if this project is going to cause you some inconvenience, Mr. Cole, but there is little that can be done. The money has already been appropriated by

Congress, the plans have been approved by the Department of the Interior, and considerable time and money have already been spent. It is the viewpoint of the current administration that the entire Western frontier should be opened up for additional settlers and not left dormant for a select few who happen to be in the cattle business. We in the Corps of Engineers have been entrusted with the responsibility to see that those objectives are met."

There was a hard glitter in Cole's eyes as he took up his reins again and shifted to a more comfortable position in the saddle. "Those few of us who happen to be in the cattle business provide damned near every scrap of meat eaten by the folks back East, Major. They have done that in the past and they will continue to do it in the future, and no four-eyed army major is going to change that. We settled this land, Major, when no one else had the guts to come out here. Our people died—men, women, and children alike— and we paid a terrible price to build what we have. There are other men just like myself further on down the line who depend on Cole Creek as much as I do. If you continue with this ridiculous project, you're going to have a hell of a lot more than just me and my men to contend with."

"Is that a threat, Mr. Cole?" Sacke said, striving for authority in his tone.

"It's more than that, son. It's a promise."

"Any interference from you will be handled through proper legal channels, sir. I have my orders and I intend to follow them out."

"Then good luck to you." Cole started to turn his horse around, but stopped and smiled down at Sacke. "I might as well let you know, you're going to have two sides to fight before this thing is settled."

A confused look crossed Sacke's face. "Two sides? I'm afraid I don't understand."

"When you were drawing your little lines and circles on those maps of yours, did you happen to follow the entire course of this proposed new creek?"

"Well, ah, not exactly. Why?"

"Because your stream is going to flow right through the center of the Sioux summer campground. They'll be up to their asses in water every time they go into their tipis."

"Then . . . then . . ." Sacke stammered, "we'll just move them."

Cole's smile broadened. "Don't think you're going to get off that easy, Major. Those people have been moved just about all they plan to be. They've got habits and traditions just like the rest of us. And one of the things they get the most riled up about is someone fooling with their burial grounds."

"Burial grounds? I have no intention to desecrate their burial grounds."

"You don't, huh?" Cole asked with a nod toward the tents spread out across the plains. "Just behind your tents there, maybe a couple hundred yards from where you're standing, is a place where the Sioux have buried their dead since the beginning of time. I wouldn't be surprised if, when your boys dug their shit trenches, they turned up a bone or two. You ain't real popular with Black Eagle right now, I suspect, and it's going to get worse."

Sacke glanced nervously in the direction indicated before looking up at Cole again. "Worse? How do you mean?"

"There's going to be a lake behind your dam, isn't there, Major?"

"Yes, of course. That's the purpose of the whole thing."

"And there's your problem. Those Sioux aren't going to appreciate having to dive down twenty feet just to visit the graves of their ancestors. Which they'll have to do, because their entire burial ground is going to be covered with water." Cole smiled again and touched the brim of his hat with two fingers while flicking spurs against his horse's flanks. "Like I said, Major, good luck."

A sinking, dejected feeling swept through Sacke as he watched the six horses gallop away. Then, turning, he scurried toward his tent, stepped inside, and began hurriedly to scrawl out the telegram to be sent to Outpost Number Nine.

EASY COMPANY

Ride the High Plains with the rough-and-tumble Infantrymen of
Outpost Nine—in John Wesley Howard's EAST COMPANY series!

LONGARM

Men love his rip-roaring,
shoot-'em-up adventures...

Women delight in his romantic exploits!
This sexy lawman is as adventurous with the ladies as
he is with his gun! Explore the exciting Old West with
one of the men who made it wild!